CHASING MY TWENTIES
AS SOMEONE'S GIRLFRIEND

CHASING MY TWENTIES

As SOMEONE'S GIRLFRIEND

A Journal Series

AMANDA BERUBE

THIS JOURNAL BELONGS TO:

Lucy

TIMEFRAME:

SEPTEMBER 2013 - JULY 2014

Entry #70

FINALLY BOUGHT A NEW NOTEBOOK.

I may have miscalculated how late my period is… I should really download an app or something so I can keep better track of it. But what I do know for certain is that it's very late.

Hunter is coming over at noon; how am I supposed to act like everything is fine when it's totally not fine? I'm freaking the fuck out.

The gyno doesn't open until tomorrow morning at seven, so there's not a damn thing I can do until then. One positive test and one negative… could the negative be a false negative or is the positive a false positive?

FUCKKKKKKKKKKKKK.

I did some research and there could be multiple reasons why this is happening; bottom line, the only for sure way to tell is by getting a blood test… which I can't do until tomorrow.

I feel so irresponsible… how could I be so stupid? I let myself get too caught up in the moment and I took it way too far. Benji and I always used condoms, so the stress level was always so low, ya know?

I should really stop being so hard on myself… it is what it is at this point. Trying to place blame isn't worth it and certainly won't help undo any potential damage that's already been done.

Hunter just walked in the door. BRB.

• • •

Just from walking in the door and kissing me, he could tell something was bothering me.

I told him I didn't want to stress him out with something until I knew for sure there was something to stress about. He told me I could tell him anything and that he's here for me no matter what… so, I spilled the big secret.

Tears filled my eyes as I worked up the courage to tell him that my period is late.

His facial expression didn't change, not even as I rambled my way through his silence.

He was such a gentleman… He wiped away my tears, pulled me in close for a hug, and told me that we would get through this together. He asked me if I had taken a test, and when I told him two, he sat up a little taller before asking me what the results were. After telling him, I immediately followed up with my plan to get over to the gyno ASAP for blood work in the morning.

I could tell his mind began to spiral just as much as mine has been… He fell quiet again until I asked him to share what he was thinking. He confessed he was a little scared but felt we should take things one day at a time.

We're on the same page about wanting a family later in life… but now? Definitely not now. Between school and work and the fact that we've only known each other for a summer… a baby is not something we need to add to the mix right now.

I will admit, he was handling things way better than I was. At least while we were face to face, he was.

We decided to focus on the fact that nothing was yet set in stone, so we ordered lunch from our usual Mexican place and stayed inside for the day. I was wondering when he was going to freak out, panic, and leave, but he remained calm and collected the entire time.

At one point, he did look me in the eyes and told me that if I was pregnant and decided to keep the baby, that nothing would change between us, and he would do everything to take care of us.

We haven't even said "I love you" yet, and here we are talking about taking care of a baby, for fuck's sake. I mean his response was everything I would have hoped for and more, it's just… this is a lot to take in, yo.

While I deeply appreciate him saying that, it didn't help the fact that I have no career right now, let alone financial stability. I have a nice job and all, but I'm a little ways away from dipping my toes into a full-blown career. I don't want to have to depend on someone else for help… I need to be stable on my own.

I of course responded with tears and told him how I wasn't sure about telling him, but he said he was glad I did because he didn't want me to have to go through this alone. We hugged and he squeezed me long enough to forget that my world was collapsing all around and underneath me.

We spent the day on the couch wrapped up in each other's arms watching movies until it was time for dinner. We had pizza and some wings delivered; my place smelled like fried buffalo chicken and pepperoni.

Hunter knows all about my writing now, so I don't feel like I have to stress about him catching me anymore. Not too sure why I was stressing about it to begin with, but baby steps, I guess.

It amazes me how supportive he is of all things Lucy related. He's a really great guy and I hope he feels supported as much as I do in our relationship. I'll make sure to say something before I give him head in a minute.

He's staying the night tonight; he doesn't want me to feel alone. We haven't said I love you yet, but his actions sure tell a different story. If I wasn't sitting next to him, I would dive into the love thing a little more, but I should really get back to our moment.

One more thing before I go.

I don't know how things are going to go tomorrow, and moving forward after, but I do know that I believe Hunter when he says he's going to support me. I hope that doesn't come back to bite me in the ass, but I have a deep feeling inside my bones that this man isn't going anywhere anytime soon. I guess only time will tell for sure.

Fingers crossed, babe.

Either way, you've got this.

Entry #71

SO, THE GOOD NEWS IS I'M NOT PREGNANT, WE DID AN INTERNAL ULTRA-sound and blood test to confirm. To add, when they did the ultrasound there was blood, so my period finally started, thank goodness. Also, internal ultrasounds are gross and way more uncomfortable than you'd expect.

The bad news is I have a cyst on my right ovary, which is more than likely the cause for the delay of my period, in addition to the other new stresses I have in my life (new relationship, being back in the work force, AND consistently working out). Basically, there are a lot of big changes my body is experiencing at once.

My gyno told me the cyst should pass on its own, but if it doesn't and seems to cause further issues, they'll need to surgically remove it. I also need to add two extra vitamins to my daily regimen. Which I guess isn't a bad thing; I'm just going to need a pill organizer at this point.

Also. Whoa. Fucking surgery, are you kidding me?! I freaked out when she told me that. Does my health insurance even cover that? Speaking of health insurance… she told me that when I turn twenty-six, I'll have to get on my own policy, I can't be on Mom's plan anymore.

The fuck? Welcome to adulthood, I guess.

She added that my recent health changes have been positive and that I need to continue with an active, healthy lifestyle for the rest of my life as this is likely to occur again. Being on birth control helps, but utilizing more natural ways to aid with it is also super helpful.

She sent me home with some pamphlets about ovarian cysts, set up an ultrasound for next Tuesday, and that was about it. I cried like a basket case when I got to my car. Mostly because I wasn't pregnant, but also because I have to deal with this now.

I just thought I was done, that's all. The car accident caused some issues that took a very long time and physical therapy to heal; it was not an easy twelve months, and so I thought once I got past that, I was done. And now this pops up two years later…

I did text Hunter right away to let him know I wasn't pregnant. He asked what it turned out to be and I told him pretty much what the gyno told me, I just explained it in a way he as a man would understand. He had to work tonight after class but told me he would come over after his shift so we could talk. He was so sweet about it and reminded me that we were in this together no matter what.

It was around lunchtime by the time I got to the office to finish up the remaining workday. I was not in the mood for anything, so I stayed at my desk and pretty much kept my head down until Austin came by to find out where I had been all morning. Apparently, we were supposed to be working on the training project today… oops.

I was honest and told him I wasn't in the mood to talk. He told me he could tell something was off, and I acknowledged that was the case but told him it wasn't something I wanted to share. He respected my space and told me he was there for me if I needed someone. I barely looked at him the entire time we spoke. I felt kind of bad about it after, but I'm sure he understood.

Mom wasn't in the office today, but she knew I had a doctor's appointment, which meant I was going to have to tell her what happened at some point. Though as far as the pregnancy scare goes, I'll keep that tiny detail to myself.

Once five o'clock hit, I could not have gotten out of that place soon enough... I sped home, put on some pajamas, and just cried. Now you find me here.

First and foremost, I'm thankful to not be pregnant. Maybe more when I'm thirty or so I'll be ready for that. But for now, I want to live my life and make up for lost time. I want to learn more about myself and really figure out who I am and who I want to be.

I've given my energy to such negative beings. Never again will I put myself in that situation.

I'm finally in a good place and I feel good, I feel almost great, better than I have in years! Do I still have some issues every now and then? Yes. Do I intentionally not write about them in hopes of avoiding giving them attention? Yes.

Should I stop doing that? Absofuckinglutely.

I feel so defeated.

Granted this is much easier to deal with than a baby, but like, this could affect me for the rest of my life. It can even affect my chances of getting pregnant in the future if the cysts become chronic and problematic.

As if having my period didn't suck enough, now this?

Mom wants to talk in the morning when I get to the office, and I really just don't want to do that. Especially not around the people we work with.

Hunter just texted that he's on his way. It's nine o'clock and I just realized I haven't eaten all day. I don't know what to do. I don't know what to eat. One small surgery isn't the end of the world; I do have health insurance, so it'll be okay. I'm just terrified at the thought of this potentially turning into a permanent thing. There has to be more that I can do to take better care of myself.

One step at a time I guess, right?

Entry #72

NOT SURE WHERE TO BEGIN, SO I GUESS I'LL TAKE IT FROM THE TOP.

Hunter came over last night and hugged me the second he walked in the door; didn't waste any time getting over to me. Tears poured out of my eyes from the very first second he held me. I couldn't help it; I just felt safe enough to let it all out, I guess. I don't know.

He reminded me that he will always be around to support me and help me in any way he can. He said he wants to make sure that I'm always taken care of.

I looked at him while rubbing my eyes and mumbled, "Why would you do that for me, why are you even so nice to me? We hardly know each other, Hunter."

He replied, "Because I care about you Lucy, I really do. I know you're going to be okay, and while it may not feel like that right now, I promise you it will be. We've only known each other for a few months, but we spent practically the entire summer together, Lucy. I've gotten to know so much about you, it's as if I've known you my entire life. It was just a matter of us finally being together for it to all make sense."

He moved in closer and kissed me softly on my forehead; joked that I was stuck with him because he wasn't going anywhere. It was a really nice conversation and I'm glad he was able to stop by.

I did finally eat after he left; I made some chicken nuggets and french fries. Granted it was way too fucking late for dinner, at least I got something in me.

Now as for this morning with Mom, that was hard. She basically said the same as Hunter, that she's here for me and how everything will be okay. Yeah, it was a little emotional given everything we've been through together, but talking to her made me feel a little better.

I was packing up my stuff to go home (Mom gave me the day off) when Austin came by; he saw that I was upset and wanted to check in.

He's such a good friend.

I got some groceries on my way home and made myself an unusually fancy lunch. I had baked salmon, mashed sweet potatoes, and roasted asparagus. Going to be a bit of a taste adjustment, but overall, it tasted pretty good. Special thanks to Hunter for the idea.

Anyway.

This period has been a bit tougher for me than most. I guess it's from the cyst; the cramps are just terrible and I'm bleeding heavier than I normally do. I guess it's a good thing Mom let me have the day off.

I do have a more positive, uplifting, and non-gross thing to share... I got my first paycheck today! Pay dates are on the first and the fifteenth of each month.

It feels so fucking incredible to be working and making money again. I'm also thankful to no longer be in retail because banking hours are so much better; we have time off for every federal holiday, which we get paid for, AND we don't work late nights and weekends. I acknowledge how lucky I am because I certainly did not have any of that before.

Granted, I still have to deal with the general public, it's mostly over the phone or email, so no more getting screamed at in front of my face. Luckily my interactions so far have been positive, minus a few here and there poking fun at my accent. Overall, it's a much better environment than what I've been in previously. I'm truly thankful and will do whatever I can to make the most out of this opportunity.

Entry #73

WEDNESDAY OCTOBER 2ND 2013

TODAY WAS A VERY BUSY DAY, AND WHILE THAT'S GREAT FOR BUSINESS, it was not great for me. I felt horrible all day, I just wanted to be in bed. This period is really taking a toll on me and now I understand why I've felt like this before; I just always thought it was normal because of how sporadic it happens. It's comforting to finally put a name to the thing that has caused me pain.

I did not go to yoga this morning; probably won't until next week once I'm feeling better. Once I got home from work, I missed a call from Scarlett while I was in the shower. She and I haven't talked in a little while.

I called her back, school's going well, otherwise she's at the restaurant any chance she can get. I told her she should probably slow down a little, but she assured me she's the happiest she's ever been. I asked her how she liked being bossed around by Benji, but she didn't seem to want to talk about it (or him), so she changed the subject and asked me how I was doing.

I thought it was strange considering gossiping is like her second language, but I didn't pry.

Speaking of strange.

Hazel texted me earlier that she and Max's brother talked about her pregnancy scare and he didn't freak out one bit. Instead, he brought up how he hopes to get married and have kids someday. She was gushing over having that conversation with him so early in their relationship, so now she's wondering if she could see herself marrying him. While I'm excited for her and hoping for the best, she might be moving a little fast. Though truthfully, I'm not one to judge given how quickly Hunter and I moved along in our relationship.

Hunter skipped work tonight to stay home and work on his sauce recipe that he has to come up with for one of his classes. He's stressed as fuck about it, but I know he'll figure it out. He always does.

As for me and my evening, I fried up a few frozen pork dumplings and watched a movie in bed. I know I'm supposed to be eating healthy, but I have zero energy to cook a full meal and that was faster than delivery.

Entry #74

TODAY WAS 'TEN-O-THREE' DAY AT WORK. A MORTGAGE LOAN APPLICATION is also called a ten-o-three, so with today being October third, it was the running joke of the day.

Hunter stayed home again to work on his recipe; he said he likes the direction he's heading in, so he should be finished with it for tomorrow's class.

Had dinner with the parents tonight; Dad grilled steaks and scallops. To pair with it, Mom made a side salad and some grilled squash and zucchini. I stayed to help clean up after and then spent the rest of my evening reading a book on the couch with a fat joint burning. This month's ounce consists of a beautiful and fluffy kush. I'm definitely enjoying it.

It's raining right now, for the third damn night in a row. Not like I have plans or anything, and I do enjoy a good rainstorm, it's just getting to be a little repetitive is all.

Oh, my yoga free trial is up on the seventh and I am definitely signing up for a membership.

Okay, time to stop deflecting and be honest with myself here.

This whole ovarian cyst thing is a lot and I put more thought into it and I'm going to start taking the vitamins the gyno suggested... what's two more? If it'll make me feel better, then it's worth the effort.

As far as the diet goes, I can work on making healthier choices... like making full meals instead of frozen stuff or ordering delivery as often as I have been lately...

The point is, I'm going to process this with an open mind and do my very best to not resort to the worst possible scenario. Yes, I understand there may be a time when I have to be more serious about making healthier food choices, but until then I choose to go at my own pace. It's a bit challenging to accept that the way I have been feeling and living is not considered normal; makes me wonder what life will be like once I get my symptoms under control.

Entry #75

WE HAD FIVE LOANS CLOSE TODAY; IT WAS A LONG AND DETAIL-ORIENTED day, but we powered through it. I'm having fun learning the "loan lingo" and piecing things together with the notes I've been studying. Makes me feel like a nerd because I'm genuinely excited to learn more.

Legit, having a great time at work. I'm enjoying the excitement and mystery that follows when you're learning something new. I haven't felt like this in ages.

I did have to work with Austin for the day, but it went fairly well. He mostly talked on the phone, and I somewhat listened while I fantasized about my future career path.

Oh! We finally had a beautiful day out, so Mom let the entire office go home early around noon once all the loans were squared away. Austin passed along in conversation that he was heading to the racetrack to do some work and could use an extra set of hands.

I bit my lip as I contemplated what to do. Until Hunter called me, so I stepped away to talk for a minute. His uncle needed him in the kitchen tonight, so we made plans for dinner at his place tomorrow after his roommate heads out of town for a few days.

While bummed, it wasn't the worst considering I still can't have sex. One more day and I should be good.

Considering my plans for the day were cancelled, I decided to go with Austin to help him out. I mean friends are allowed to hang out with each other and I figured there would be other people there.

Well, I was totally wrong, it was just us.

We talked and he mentioned there's a girl in our yoga class that he has a thing for.

I knew something was up when he started wearing cologne.

I told him he should go for it and ask her out, but he was nervous. I reminded him of qualities of his that women would find attractive; he seemed to get a kick out of that.

While I was clueless to what we were doing, I still managed to assist fairly well on the brake job he was doing.

Maybe one day I'll be able to get behind the wheel of one of those things...

After about an hour or so, I headed out and grabbed a sandwich for lunch on the way home. Sat outside on the balcony with some music playing and enjoyed the moment.

BTW, so ready to get back to yoga and on a more regular schedule. Plus, the ultrasound is on Tuesday and I'm looking forward to moving on from this. I can't handle surgery right now; I won't even go down that rabbit hole. It's not worth it.

I took advantage of the nice weather and rode around the neighborhood on my bike for a bit. Took a few different turns that I normally wouldn't take, but I enjoyed getting lost on the side streets.

I eventually found my way onto a more familiar street, the treehouse to be exact, but some kids were swinging on the swing set, so I went home. Put in a good six miles, all within forty-five minutes.

I took my time showering; shaved, did a face mask, eye mask, and moisturized my whole body when I got out. It was refreshing and I think my body needed to recharge like that. I was in no mood to cook dinner; I had exhausted what remaining energy I had left on what was a very peaceful bike ride under the sun.

… But I'm supposed to be eating a bit healthier so I can take better care of myself… Ugh, adulting sucks.

I know it's for the best and I want my body to feel good, but I guess certain things could be better… fuck, you're right. It's just food. You can do it.

I need to be easier on myself. I'm only twenty-five, I'm still learning how to be on my own and having to be responsible for things I never thought about before. I'll figure it out in my own time.

Once my hair was dry enough to justify going out in public, I threw on enough clothes for a quick grocery run. I grabbed the essentials with some extra vegetables, baked chips, and some sugar-free chocolate chip cookies to try.

As I was getting ready to check out, I ended up in line behind Max.

To be honest, I was not expecting to see him ever again. Especially not dressed the way I was…

He casually mentioned how happy Hazel makes his brother before telling me how good he thought I looked. Like, what?

I went home and made some grilled chicken with roasted sweet pota-toes, bacon, and brussels sprouts. Yes, I used Hunter's recipe again. And yes, it was nice to have a tasty, and healthy, meal. Very thankful to have him help me with all of this. Cooking is just not a huge thing for me so I'm glad it's his.

I got myself together and laid in bed with some TV show playing in the background. Hunter just got home from work and sent me a picture of him in the shower.

Reallyy looking forward to seeing him tomorrow.

Entry #76

HUNTER TOLD ME HE LOVED ME.

We were in his kitchen, and I was sitting on the counter while he was standing over at the stove cooking his new sauce for me (that his instructors loved by the way).

I was wearing one of his T-shirts with thigh-high socks and he was in his sweatpants, shirtless.

When he was finished, he brought a spoonful over for me to taste. It was some kind of tomato mushroom crème sauce, and it tasted amazing. My face immediately lit up as I told him I loved it just as I was staring right into his eyes.

He smiled and said thank you before turning back around to face the stove. I refreshed our wine glasses while he plated dinner.

He casually mentioned how much he loves cooking for me, then turns around and walks back over and places his hands on the counter space around me, boxing me in. Our bodies were so close together, yet barely touching.

Our eyes were locked; he's smiling all calm, cool, and collected, and I'm over here hoping I'm not smiling too hard because of how much I was gushing over this moment we were having…

What can I say, I was under his spell.

He moved in closer to me and rubbed the tip of his nose back and forth against mine. Our eyes were closed now, and our lips were just barely touching when he whispered, "I love you, Lucy."

Our faces were so close to each other's, I know he felt me smile.

I whispered back, "I love you too, Hunter."

When our lips finally touched, I wrapped my legs around his waist, and he carried me over to his bed.

So glad I have moved on from my fear of being picked up… at least for the most part. It still gets me from time to time but I've learned to give it up in the moment and dwell on it later. May not be the best practice, but at least I get to enjoy the moment instead of ruining it with my negative thoughts.

Rewinding before I ruin this moment by talking about my body image demons.

So, he carries me over to his bed and lowers me down so I'm flat on my back. I leaned forward and pulled off my shirt; he slid my underwear off. Then he pulled me in close to his face and dove right into my pussy with those damn juicy lips of his.

How did I get so fucking lucky?

• • •

I totally came on his face.

He stood up and wiped his mouth with his forearm. Paused, then looked at me and told me he was ready to be inside of me.

He took his time getting undressed. Meanwhile I'm lying on the bed with my legs spread open, dripping wet, just waiting for him to stick his dick in me.

He teased me with the tip, then started off slowly before he picked up in speed.

We tried reverse cowgirl. A girlfriend perk he unlocked.

It was a little awkward to start, we definitely giggled a good bit, but when we got it, we fucking got it. Real talk about feeling stuffed.

Oh, we totally forgot about dinner. It was cold by the time we were done, but at least he turned the stove off, so nothing burned. He heated it up really quick while I looked for a movie for us to watch.

Dinner was amazing and by the end of the movie, we were spooning. I was the little spoon.

He's always so warm, it's got to be all that hair on his body.

Neither one of us wanted to move, but we had a nice, cozy bed to lay in as opposed to this much smaller couch we were on. We cleaned up just enough to feel good about leaving some dishes behind and headed to bed. He rolled us a joint while I freshened up for the night.

I sat between his legs with my back pressed against his torso; he was sitting up, leaning against the headboard. We passed a joint back and forth and talked about anything that came to mind.

At one point, I leaned my hand back and felt up the side of his face as I pulled mine in closer to his.

I thought I was going to burst inside. Something about that just felt so intimate, so familiar. I loved every second of it. Really digging this fall/winter seasonal beard he has going on, it's so sexy. He was pretty clean shaven in the summer, so this is like a totally different side of him.

The love vibes were strong, and I wished it didn't have to end. I mean we did eventually end up falling asleep, but not until after we had sex one more time.

When we woke up for the day, it was only a little after eight, so we laid in bed for another hour until we decided on some breakfast.

I ran to get us some coffee and he made us bacon and Cinnabons. His place smelled like cinnamon and vanilla when I returned, it was great.

We sat at the table together and talked about the day ahead. He was off work, and I had nothing planned.

It was beautiful outside, but without the sun shining directly on you, it was a little chilly. We decided to go for a walk and found ourselves stopping by the treehouse for a bit. It's been a while since we've been over there.

We laid down next to each other and looked up at the sky. He pulled out his earbuds and we each put one in our ear. He played some music on low, and we talked. Almost like we had our own playlist playing in the background. It was romantic, and it was a huge turn on.

He changed the pace of the music when I decided to surprise him with some head, had some hardcore rock going on or something, I don't know, but it set a nice rhythm. I got on top of him after and rode him until we heard people, so we of course stopped, freaked the fuck out for a second, then laughed as we climbed down and headed back to his place to see that those people were only just passing by, walking in the street.

For context: this treehouse we go to is literally in a field with two old swings attached to the side. It's not like we were in a park or anything, but getting caught still would have been gross and embarrassing.

Anyway, we went back to his place and finished where we left off. Only this time we were on the couch, and yes, we kept the earbuds in. It really added to the experience. Totally crossing it off the nonexistent bucket list.

We had leftovers for lunch and spent the rest of the afternoon into the evening on the couch, cuddled up watching movies.

Fuck I never texted the parents that I wouldn't be at breakfast this morning.

I'm sure they know about Hunter; at least now more than ever they have a reason to suspect something.

I just checked my phone for the first time today and I didn't have any messages or missed calls from them, so I guess we're all good.

Anyway, back to Hunter.

Still feeling pretty full from lunch, we decided to skip dinner and call it a night since we both have to be up early tomorrow. Now that we're on the "I love you" level, saying goodbye feels harder than ever. Yes, even though we live only a few doors down, it still feels like we're on opposite ends of the world.

When I got home, I nibbled on a chicken wrap I had in the fridge and got right to business.

I LOVE YOU?!

Seven months ago, I wasn't looking for a man, and now here I am in love with my weed dealer.

It is really good to finally say it out loud because let's be honest, I've been feeling it for a lot longer than I will admit.

I'm trying to narrow it down in my head to when I first fell in love with him, but honestly, I can't pinpoint something that may have been there from the start? I don't know, I'm not saying I fell in love with him at first sight or anything, but the feelings were strong from the very beginning and there is no denying that.

Was it the cooking class he invited me to? I mean that was the night we broke one of our rules and started sleepovers. IDK.

Hunter seems like the kind of guy who respects my independence as much as I respect his. We build each other up, and I'm excited to see where this goes.

He just texted me, "Goodnight baby, I love you. I miss you already."

How did I get so fucking lucky?!

Entry #77

I WAS ALL SMILES AT YOGA THIS MORNING, HAD AUSTIN BUZZING IN MY ear asking what was up, but I didn't say anything. The drive home was peaceful despite a little traffic; however, I took a little too long to get ready this morning and was almost late for work. And by almost, I mean I wasn't ten to fifteen minutes early like I usually am. Oh well.

Oh! I signed up for the yoga membership; it's only thirty dollars a week, which is not bad at all for unlimited classes. Now that I'm a month in, I've noticed my body feels a bit more relaxed and flexible. I know Hunter has noticed a difference too.

Austin told me he was glad to see me feeling better but was ready to finish up this training program he and I were tasked with. He expects to be done with it by the end of the week so he can start focusing on his loan officer test. We got a good amount of work done today; just tightening up some workflow steps is really all that's left. The idea is to create directions those with no industry experience, like me, could follow. Hence why he and I were partnered up together.

Mom threw us a curve ball by the way.

She wants Austin and I to fly up to one of the lenders we work with in Chicago because they have two-day training classes that could benefit us. A processor intro training course for me and loan officer studies for him. We leave Tuesday night and return Friday morning. Yup, this week.

I wasn't thrilled and I expressed that very clearly, but it was already done. The fact that I was going to have to travel somewhere new with Austin and spend the night somewhere with him for three nights did not sound like such a fun time. Especially right after Hunter and I just said "I love you" for the first time… I want to be here with Hunter, not in Chicago with another guy for work.

Austin and I didn't talk for the rest of the day. We had loan stuff we had to handle and some other things to prepare for the upcoming days ahead since we'll be tied up in training classes and travel.

I mean, it is exciting having your company fly you out to somewhere you've never been before so you can improve yourself and explore the area in your free time… all at their expense.

I should really stop complaining and embrace the opportunity.

• • •

I called Hunter on my way home from work and told him the details. He's going to miss me but is excited for me and hopes I have a good time. Said he'll see me Friday night and that he'll take the night off work so we can spend it together.

There is nothing sexier than a man rearranging his schedule to spend time with you. I bet it's because he's older than me and has his life together. As for me, I'm still fucking up along the way as I find my place in this world. I'm glad I have him by my side to catch me if I fall.

He offered to cook dinner, so I had him send me the grocery list so I could stock the fridge. I'll run to the store on my way home from the airport on Friday so it's all fresh.

He had to get back to work and I had to figure out dinner myself. I wasn't starving, so I decided to take my time and make jambalaya. I swear it's my new favorite dish. The recipe I used calls for kielbasa sausage, chicken, shrimp, rice, peppers, chicken stock, okra, tomato sauce, and miscellaneous herbs and spices. Took about a little over an hour to cook and it was close to eight by the time it was done. A little later than normal, but totally worth it.

Believe it or not, I found this recipe on my own. I'll have to make it for Hunter one night so I can show off to him in the kitchen.

Oh, fuck.

My ultrasound is in the morning… totally forgot all about the cyst. Now I can't go to yoga and that would have been really nice to do before a few days of travel.

Fuck. What if I need surgery and can't go on my trip?

What if I need surgery?

I really don't want to go through that again…

This is one of my ovaries we're talking about. If something goes wrong or an ovary is damaged, that could hurt my chances of ever having kids of my own someday.

Holy fucking shit this is serious.

Entry #78

THE FOLLOW-UP ULTRASOUND WENT OKAY. SUCKS HAVING A WAND SHOVED into me poking around, but it was over quickly. I guess.

The cyst is very much still there, but it decreased in size enough to no longer need to worry about having it surgically removed.

God heard my prayers.

I was so fucking scared.

We flew out this afternoon around four fifteen, so we got off work early to pack and head to the airport. Unfortunately, Hunter was still in class, so I didn't get to see him before I left. This is the first time we've been apart since we've met, and we just said "I love you" for the first time. Talk about the timing…

Austin and I sat next to each other on the plane. We had a two-and-a-half-hour flight ahead of us. I was a little nervous; this was my longest flight and flying makes me a little anxious to begin with. He caught on and was a gentleman about it, helped distract me with conversation. He had been to the city we were going to before, so he knew all the hotspots we should go to. He talked about the time he attended the classes I'm about to take and thinks I'll enjoy them. We shall see.

We landed and got to the hotel sometime in the evening, around eight. I checked in with Hunter while Austin handled the front desk. Turns out our rooms were right across the hall from each other. How convenient.

We dropped off our luggage and ordered a car to this Asian place Austin raved about. Dinner was delicious, just as good as he described. And as far as the drinks go, they were indeed very strong. Maybe the traveling heightened the alcohol intensity a little, I don't know.

We decided to walk back to the hotel since it wasn't too far away. It was a little chilly out, but nothing the alcohol couldn't warm up. Plus, I brought my nice brown jacket and a scarf, so that helped. I looked very cute actually—wish I snapped a picture.

The walk back took about fifteen minutes, it wasn't too bad. Honestly, I needed it after the meal I had just eaten; it was very filling and the desire to get up and move around was strong.

We talked about life and how things are going at work and outside of work. He asked if I would finally tell him what was up with me yesterday morning, and since we're technically friends, friends don't keep secrets, so I told him. It felt a little awkward given our questionable lustful past, but he was happy for me.

He brought up the girl from yoga class again. I told him he should go for it, but he still isn't sure if that's what he needs right now. I reminded him of how much work he's done for himself over the summer and that maybe it's time to lighten up and start enjoying life now.

We made it back to the hotel, said goodnight, and went our separate ways. It's an odd feeling knowing he's sleeping right across the hall from me. He's so close, I can't help but feel a little curious.

Not that I would do anything about it, just curious because if I was single, who knows what kind of mess he and I would be getting into right now.

Hunter and I got to talk again; by the time I was settling down he was just getting off work, so we video chatted for a bit. He admitted he was a little jealous that I was traveling somewhere with another guy; I let him know he had nothing to worry about and brought up the idea that he and I should take a trip of our own sometime. He was all for it.

We called it a night around midnight my time (we're an hour apart). I have class from nine to five tomorrow and Thursday, and we only get like thirty minutes for lunch each day. Talk about information overload.

Entry #79

OKAY, I'M STILL A LITTLE TIPSY, SO FOLLOW ALONG WITH ME.

Day two was no less of an information overload than yesterday. Except today I had some breakfast beforehand and that really made me feel better about myself, I felt more focused and attentive.

The flight home leaves tomorrow at around eleven thirty in the morning, so Austin and I decided to cheers to hard work and drink a little extra tonight. This time we ate at one of the hotel restaurants, so we didn't have to wander off too far. We ate some Mexican food, so we had big drinks and tons of chips and salsa before and after dinner. Something about alcohol, chips, and salsa, man. Tastes so good.

We finally called it a night and found ourselves alone in the elevator on the way back up to our rooms.

Both of us were feeling good about ourselves but keeping it to ourselves. As soon as the doors shut, we immediately fell silent as we stood in opposite corners of the elevator. The elevator walls were covered in mirrors, so while we avoided making eye contact and looking in the other's general direction, I did catch him glancing at me in the mirror's reflection.

If you recall, the last time we were drinking together was at that one restaurant with his friends where we found ourselves intertwined in a basement bathroom sucking each other's faces… so I guess given the circumstances the silence was justified.

When the elevator got to our floor, we stepped out one at a time and stood side by side walking down the hall together. When we got to our rooms, we stood in the center of the hall, confirmed what time we had to meet in the morning to get to the airport on time, and then went our separate ways. He shut his door behind him, and I shut mine behind me.

The silence was super awkward and really confusing because it wasn't weird until we were alone in the elevator.

He still can't have feelings for me, can he?

BRB Hunter's calling. I'm tipsy so I'm going to talk him into some phone sex.

Entry #80

SATURDAY OCTOBER 12ᵀᴴ 2013

I HAD BREAKFAST YESTERDAY MORNING AT THE HOTEL BEFORE AUSTIN AND I got to the airport around nine. The flight back home felt like it was taking forever.

He slept and I read a book, though I mostly fantasized about what my night was going to look like.

I didn't get home until close to four o'clock. Food shopping was rough, but I got some sweets, so it was worth it.

Fast forward. I unpacked and showered, got myself together for the night, and Hunter came by around seven. I don't know why but he brought me some flowers, as if cooking us dinner wasn't enough. He's so sweet!

I sat on the counter in my usual spot sipping wine while he did all the cooking. He didn't want me lifting a finger… this man spoils me. We ate on the couch with a Halloween movie playing in the background and just enjoyed each other's company. We talked about our weeks and what we had planned for the weekend. He's off in the morning but has to work in the afternoon, so he's spending the night.

By the end of the movie, I was definitely a bit drunk, as was he. We didn't bother cleaning up the kitchen, but we did fool around on the couch for a hot minute.

He met me in the middle when I was returning to the living room after dropping off our plates. He kissed me up and down my neck, and I his. Bodies now intertwined, we managed to undress each other as we made our way over to the couch. He laid me down and traced his tongue all up and down my chest, bit my nipples on his way down to my thighs.

Dude, he ravished my pussy. There's no other way for me to describe what he did to me. It's like my little time away intensified the craving we already have for each other.

We moved to my bedroom and I got on top of him. I stopped when he was about to cum so I could give him head. He was lying on the bed to start, then we switched it up so he could stand and I could be on my knees.

He fucked my mouth up until he was ready to cum. As he's pulling out, he tells me to open wide and stick my tongue out.

I obeyed.

Our eyes were fixed on each other's the entire time he's finishing in my mouth and all over my boobs.

I don't know what perk he unlocked, but damn.

Sex that intense called for some weed, so we cleaned up and settled in bed before falling asleep together.

• • •

We woke up this morning and took a shower together. Washing each other's bodies with hot, soapy water is so damn sexy, we can't keep our hands to ourselves. It's impossible.

He cooked us breakfast while I cleaned up last night's mess. Thank goodness for dishwashers and teamwork.

I wasn't feeling hungover, but definitely needed some coffee. It was a nice day out, so we went for a walk on this trail at a park. We rolled a joint before we left, so once we knew we were alone, we sparked up and kept on our way; did about three miles in total. The weather was perfect… the sunshine was strong enough to keep us warm from the cool breeze, so we didn't even work up a sweat.

Walking under the trees along the path felt calming, almost as if nature had us wrapped up in a bubble all safe and sound from the outside world.

We crossed over a little brown drawbridge, and on the other side was a small lake with some turtles resting on rocks and ducks swimming around. There was a bench nearby, so we decided to take a break and enjoy the view. After a few minutes, we checked the time and decided to head back so we could have enough time for lunch before Hunter had to get to work.

We grabbed sandwiches and took them back to my place, ate outside on the balcony so we could continue to enjoy the weather. He still teases me from time to time about the fact that I bought a purple table, but oh well.

After he left, I decided to do laundry and clean the place up a bit. I made tuna casserole for dinner and now I'm catching up in here after enjoying a much-needed bubble bath. I sprinkled some dried rose petals in the tub and lit a candle, it was nice and relaxing. I haven't taken a bath in a while, let alone set the mood for myself. I have to remember that just because I have a man in my life doesn't mean I need to stop taking care of myself and my needs.

I put on a movie and I'm texting with Hazel. She's hanging out with Max's brother and mentioned Max has a girl over. It doesn't faze me at all; he was fun while it lasted and honestly nothing tops what Hunter and I have going on.

Entry #81

SUNDAY OCTOBER 13ᵀᴴ 2013

HAZEL INVITED ME AND HUNTER TO THE PUMPKIN PATCH WITH HER AND Max's brother tonight. There's a haunted hayride and some food trucks she wants to check out.

I did my food shopping and food prep for the week while Hunter was working. He came by around five-ish all showered and smelling amazing, like some exotic ocean or something. It was such an intense smell, I was totally wrapped around his finger. He was wearing jeans, a hat, and a deep-red T-shirt. I was wearing black leggings with my new winter boots I just got and a gray hoodie.

We met Hazel and her boyfriend at the pumpkin patch. While we waited for the haunted hayride to open up, we made use of the remaining daylight checking out the food trucks before venturing out on a search for the perfect pumpkins.

Hazel and her boyfriend had asked us to take a picture of them together, and it was totally cute, they look so good together. Then they asked if Hunter and I wanted one and we laughed, realizing we haven't taken any photos of us together yet. I don't know why I was so nervous to take a picture with him for the first time, but I'm so glad we did. We do look good together and now I have a new picture for my phone's lock screen.

Also, I look so short standing next to him. I think it's fucking great and I love that he's taller than me. I like that he towers over me.

By the time we put our pumpkins away, it was time to get in line for the hayride. About twenty-five minutes later it was our turn, and damn, was it creepy. I'm not a fan of being scared and I especially hate jump scares. I held onto Hunter's arm literally the entire time. Poor Hazel screamed her head off at one point, it was hilarious. I guess she's really into Halloween and spooky, scary stuff. She's the best.

However many minutes later, the ride was over, and we parted ways. I wanted to thank Hunter for being such a gentleman and for protecting me by riding him in the front seat of his jeep, but the parking lot was a little too crowded and I'm not trying to get arrested, so I gave him road head on the way home instead.

He came inside and we fooled around for a bit until he had to leave, because tomorrow's Monday and we're adults with responsibilities.

While I'm excited for yoga, I'm more excited to wrap up this training program Austin and I have been working on. We got distracted with the training classes, so I hope by midweek we can get this thing finished so I can move on to other things.

Entry #82

WE HAD A SUB AT YOGA THIS MORNING, SO THE VIBE WASN'T THE TYPICAL that I'm used to. It was refreshing to see a new side of things, I'll give it that.

Austin and I finished up the training project early. Mom said she'd review and get back to us by Friday. I'm glad to finally be moving on from it; it seems to have dragged on for way longer than expected.

We parted ways, so I finally had some time to organize all the things I learned from last week's training; so that's how I spent the rest of my workday.

When I got home, I just had some leftovers for dinner, wasn't really in the mood to eat much.

I think I may just go to bed early. I'm just looking forward to a new day tomorrow.

I don't know man, just feeling a weird mood today. I think I'm just worried the other foot is going to drop and I'm going to lose everything I've received this summer. All good things eventually come to an end, right?

I mean think about it, what if I was pregnant? What kind of world would I be bringing a child into… I'm not married and I'm fresh at a new job in an industry I'm sometimes questioning is the right one for me… For the record, I am thankful to have a job and a place to live with a low housing payment, but still. When I have a baby, I want it to be with my husband in our home together… not like this. Not while I'm trying to figure out who I am and what I want to do with my life.

A baby needs stability, they need access to whatever it is they need when they need it.

A baby needs a lot of things that I cannot provide right now.

Plus, like, I'm finally doing things for myself. I'm enjoying this life of mine the way it is right now.

◆ ◆ ◆

I think that's enough for tonight. Hopefully I will be in a better mood tomorrow.

Entry # 83

I SLEPT IN SO I MISSED YOGA, AND THEN I COULDN'T FIND ANY CLOTHES to wear that I felt comfortable in. The only thing that seemed to work was an oversized sweater, some leggings, and boots. Not sexy boots, I'm talking the warm, thick, winter kind of boots.

I rushed through getting myself together to hurry up and cook so I could at least have breakfast.

Made my coffee to go, only to spill it on myself when I got to work because I had too many things in my hand: my backpack, a bag of water bottles for the day with my lunch, plus my work laptop, because for whatever fucking reason, I take it home with me almost every single day. Some days I mess around on it when I'm home, but I should really learn to separate the two. I spent enough free time over the summer studying; it's time to let the hands-on work experience teach me now.

Today I will stop bringing my work computer home with me. Whatever doesn't get done today that can wait for tomorrow will wait. No more bullshit.

For real this time.

As for the coffee spill, it wasn't the worst looking stain in the world, but it wasn't the prettiest either. I was wearing a navy-blue sweater and the spill happened when I was sitting in the car, so luckily it spilled towards

"

the bottom end of my sweater. When I got to work and finally put all my shit down, I headed to the bathroom to clean it up.

We had a buyer, that was clear to close and closing on Friday, put in his two weeks' notice at his current job to start with a new company after closing, and we found out during the final verification of employment that gets done right before closing.

This means the loan is no longer clear to close and is now subject to verification of the new employment information to see if the guy still qualifies to buy the house… three days before closing! What a fucking nightmare.

The loan officer was nearly speechless… we've all heard the lectures that have been passed on to this first-time home buyer, but for some reason he didn't listen.

Nobody knows anything about the new employment situation, so we have to hope and pray he still qualifies. But most importantly, the seller of the house will allow a closing extension. They too have a home they are trying to purchase, so now it will delay that closing as well… What a fucking nightmare.

Despite the day's drama, I enjoyed my lunch, so that was a nice positive given this random funk I've been in. I made some crispy chicken tender ranch wraps with American cheese wrapped in lettuce. They were fucking delicious.

Man, I was so bummed out this morning that I almost forgot today was payday!

I talked to Hunter on his way to work while I cooked some dinner. He suggested Mongolian beef and broccoli, so I whipped some up while he walked me through how to make it.

Good news is he is taking off work tomorrow night so he can chill after class. I'm glad he's getting a break.

He offered to make lobster mac and cheese if I wanted some company; of course I accepted. I don't know how cooking a fancy meal is him taking a break, but I'll let him have at it if it'll make him happy. He said he would come by around seven so he could game a little before he comes over, which gave me time to clean up my place and set the mood a little.

Entry # 84

I GOT UP ON TIME THIS MORNING AND MADE IT TO YOGA; THAT REALLY helped me start my day off better. I guess it's true when they say a morning routine can really shape the rest of your day.

Guess I need to whoop my ass into a more disciplined routine... Shit, I really do, I feel I've been slacking.

So, I wore heels and a skirt to work today.

After I showered and blow-dried my hair, I put on some makeup and managed to not totally fuck it up. My hair had a bounce to it and my eyes had a glimmer that I caught in the mirror as I was heading out the front door.

When I got to work, Mom caught notice of me and told me I looked like I was glowing. That made me feel nice considering how lame and down I've been feeling. She also added that she loves the training materials Austin and I put together and is proud of the work we've done.

Two for two, baby.

Hazel and I have been doing a little shopping here and there lately, so I decided to finally try out this look. I was wearing a maroon-colored, long-sleeved V-neck sweater, a fitted black skirt, and my black heels.

The rest of the day flew by, which was nice. When I got home, I burned some candles and put on some TV show to play in the background. When Hunter came by, I was still dressed in my work clothes. He put the groceries down on the counter and led us to my room so he could further explore my outfit for a few minutes.

He totally likes it when I get dressed up. I love it.

He sat on the edge of my bed with his feet planted on the floor, told me to take off my underwear and sit on his lap with my back turned to him. He's so much taller than I am, my feet could barely touch the floor underneath me.

He reached under my shirt and unhooked my bra before sliding his hands around front and cupping my boobs. With a gentle squeeze, he moved them around in his hands in a circular motion. From the second he unhooked my bra, I was feeling relaxed and refreshed.

He lifted my shirt up and over my head before moving all my hair over to my left shoulder. He kissed up, down, and all around the right side of my neck so gently and slowly, it was totally giving me goosebumps.

His hands moved from my boobs down the curves of my body, eventually reaching my pussy. He wets his fingers with his mouth before teasing my clit with his thumb, it was totally working. Then he pulls away and sucks on his fingers before putting them inside me. His other hand was over my mouth to stop me from screaming. I came so hard it's not even funny yo, my stomach was hurting it was so intense. We finished with my legs over his shoulders and this time his fingers were inside my mouth.

It's good to know he likes skirts; I should really consider adding miniskirts to my lingerie collection.

Anyway, we finally ate dinner sometime close to nine. He let me keep the leftovers for lunch tomorrow, so I let him have the leftover Mongolian beef so he could have a home-cooked meal instead of work food for lunch tomorrow. That's the first time he's eaten something I've cooked, though remember it was his recipe. I should cook him something of my own sometime.

His friend with the boat is having a party Friday night, so that'll be fun. Hazel and her boyfriend will be there. She and I will get with the girlfriends' group about making a punch for the night. Hunter said he can take off Saturday morning, but he has to pull a half for Friday night, so he and I will be a little late, which is fine.

Well, I've washed my face, brushed my teeth, and now I'm all caught up in here, so I think I'm going to head to bed. Glad to be feeling a little bit better and I hope it continues, because I hate being in a funk. Writing definitely helps; I bet that's why I do this journal thing. I mean it's not like I plan to publish them at any point.

OMG.

Could you imagine being a published author? What if one day you got paid to write? Would you do it? Could you see a future in writing instead of mortgages?

Is the finance industry just as stable as the writing industry? I feel like they would both have their ups and downs depending on the market and economy, like any other would. I mean technically I could always stick with mortgages while I strengthen my writing and start applying for those kinds of jobs to get a feel for the industry.

Yo. What if I got a writing job that I could do from home? I mean I already have an office that's begging to be used...

The other catch is the money. Sales can have the potential for high earnings, but it's very demanding and does not come at an easy price. Writing salaries appear to be across the board but would be a pay cut from what I'm making now to start out. I mean my rent is very little, so this could be the perfect opportunity to see what's out there in that realm...

At the end of the day, I'm in an entry-level position whichever way I choose to go. Shouldn't I take advantage of that kind of opportunity? I kind of feel like maybe I should. But maybe I just won't tell anyone for right now, so it doesn't become a thing.

Entry #85

THE LOAN OFFICER WITH THAT LOAN TROUBLE FROM EARLIER IN THE WEEK found out some positive news about the borrower's new job, so it seems all will work out. Thank goodness, because that would have sucked for a lot of people if the deal was going to fall through. This is why people should be honest and up-front about everything when buying a home, or anything major for that matter. I mean buying a home is the biggest purchase of your life—how could you NOT be totally honest?

End of rant.

Mom signed off on the training materials Austin and I put together, so we can finally put that project past us. He announced he will now be working on getting his loan officer license, so he's excited for that. I'm curious to learn/hear more about that at a later time.

I stopped by the liquor store on the way home and dropped the stuff off at Hazel's so they didn't have to wait for me to arrive to make the punch. I stayed for about an hour so we could plan outfits before Max's brother arrived to pick her up.

I wore my bootcut flared jeans, a light purple top, and a gray, cozy cardigan with sneakers. Hunter was wearing blue jeans, his hat, and a solid navy-green T-shirt. Not to sound biased or anything, but damn do we look good standing next to each other.

He and I had a few drinks; he stopped at some point so he could drive us home. I wouldn't say I stopped, but I slowed down a little. The punch the girls and I made was stronger than we all expected; that was a fun surprise.

Hunter and I walked along the beach dodging waves, holding hands this time. Crazy to look back on where we were when we last found ourselves walking on this beach (when our pinkies just almost barely touched).

We soon headed back over to the fire; it was getting to be a little chilly out.

I was feeling myself now that we were warming up and sitting still, Hunter on the other hand was ready to tap out and head home. We left about twenty minutes later and grabbed some burgers for dinner on the way home.

We went back to my place and put on a Halloween movie to watch while we ate. He was ballsy and lit a joint... of course I took a hit or two and about fifteen minutes later I was regretting it because scary movies and smoking weed, let alone cross buzzing, do not go very well together. I got up to clean and distracted myself for a few minutes before returning to the living room. He offered to turn the movie off, but I didn't want to be a buzz kill so I just cuddled up next to him and held on to his arm the whole time.

Eventually my buzz went away and the movie ended, so we moved into my bed, and while he looked for another movie to watch, I washed my face, brushed my teeth, and wrote in here. I love how he supports my writing and gives me the space I need for it. Granted he may peek over his shoulder a time or two; I think he's looking at me doing my thing more than he's looking at what I'm writing. Kind of like the way I watch him while he cooks.

Entry #86

SATURDAY OCTOBER 19TH 2013

HUNTER JUST LEFT FOR WORK AFTER WE HAD SOME LUNCH, AND I DON'T know what to do with myself for the rest of the day. It is surprisingly warm out, so maybe I should go for a bike ride. I do need to go food shopping though… eh, I'll just do that tomorrow. I'm going to go ride my bike while it's nice out.

◆ ◆ ◆

I hit up the bike path and it was totally the right decision to make.

I saw a few yellow butterflies floating around, and instead of music, I listened to the sounds of nature and managed to quiet my mind enough to appreciate the wind blowing through my hair. I was in my own protected world.

Hazel wanted to swing by tonight for an impromptu girl's night, so I headed home to shower and get ready. We ordered Chinese and pizza, crushed three bottles of wine together, and watched Halloween movies from our childhood all night.

She's asleep on the couch right now. She fell asleep during one of the movies, so I cleaned up and let her be. Now here you find me.

Been texting with Hunter all night; he's gaming with Scarlett's brother and his roommate. They're doing some Halloween squad challenge or something, who knows really. He's off tomorrow night so he'll be coming over for dinner. Which reminds me, I haven't been to Sunday breakfast in a hot minute with the parents, so I guess I have to get up early for that. I'll bring Hazel with me so they can get to know one another.

$\mathcal{E}$ntry #87

TO OUR SURPRISE, HAZEL AND I WERE NOT AS HUNGOVER AS WE EX-pected we might be.

Breakfast with the parents went well; they were excited to meet some-one new I've met here.

We stayed for about an hour and then Hazel headed home so she could get ready for her day ahead.

I got myself together and did my food shopping for the week. For lunch I made a grilled chicken sandwich with shredded mozzarella cheese, sliced pickles, and Italian dressing on a toasted sub. SO good.

I smoked a joint while I put away my groceries and cooked lunch. Eating a full meal sobered me up, so I finished the rest while I rolled a new one for later.

Hunter swung by a little after five. He went home to shower first, so he smelled really good when he got to me. I don't know how to describe the smell, but I can say that it drives me fucking wild. It's some type of French ocean scent or something, I think is what he said.

By the time he arrived I was stoned, yo. AKA handsy. Combine that with him smelling as good as he did and that was it. I got down on my knees while he stood against the kitchen counter and gave him head while he smoked so he could feel as good as I was feeling. Then he ate me out on the countertop to combat the cotton mouth he had, before we finished on the table with my legs over his shoulders and his hand wrapped around my throat.

It's the fucking cologne yo, I'm telling you.

So, he actually let me help him cook this time! We made steak, scallops, roasted asparagus, and baked potatoes. He handled the steak and scallops, I did the sides.

It was kind of fun cooking beside him. While it's nice to sit back and watch, it's a lot more fun to be in on the action with him.

We decided to eat dinner out on the balcony because of how nice it felt outside; something different, it was nice. We both cleaned up before he went on his way. He's got a busy week ahead of him school wise, so he needs to rest and be focused.

After he left, I got myself together and now I'm in bed. It may be the high from our evening together, but I'm totally fantasizing about him and I living together. Granted we've only known each other for four months; I feel like I've known him for so much longer. Not that I'm saying I would move in with him anytime soon, I'm enjoying having my own space for the first time ever, it's just nice to think about is all. I'm curious what it would be like since we have so much fun together now. Then again, maybe it's so fun because we have our own places to return to at the end of the day? #anxiety

Entry #88

MONDAY OCTOBER 21ˢᵀ 2013

YOGA WENT WELL THIS MORNING AND AUSTIN SEEMED TO BE SUPER FLIRTY with his new friend. When he came into work, I asked him what the scoop was; he said they've been texting a lot and he is going to ask her out.

Took him long enough.

He gushed to me about his new crush, he seems to really like her. I'm happy for him, he deserves someone to share his life with. Her name is Chloe… Chloe and Austin, that sounds like a love story waiting to happen.

She's really pretty too; total opposite looking from Austin. She's got long blonde hair, blue eyes, and has that rich kid, Southern belle vibe going on. She has no visible tattoos and wears a cross around her neck. It's like he's her darkness and she's his light.

I'm intrigued to see where this goes.

Back to business.

I had a relatively busy day; it was nice to be back to my normal work routine. It got so busy, I ate lunch at my desk, and next thing I knew, it was time to leave for the day. Today legit flew by, it was very nice.

On my way home, Scarlett called me to check in. I was surprised to hear from her. She's been so busy with school and working at the restaurant, I didn't think I'd hear from her again so soon.

She seemed to have a skittish attitude talking with me tonight; it was strange and very different from the last time we talked. I asked her if she was okay, and she assured me she was… Maybe she's just stressed and needs to take some time off. I told her to take a break this week, so we'll see if she actually does it or not.

Hunter took the night off work tonight and tomorrow so he can get some extra studying done. He's nearly six months away from graduating and I can tell he's ready to move on. My period started, so it's a good thing he's tied up this week. Oh, I finally downloaded a cycle tracking app—I'm curious to see how easier life is by tracking my cycle.

Literally kicking myself for not ever doing this sooner, but oh well. Birth control helps, but seeing it digitally and having reminders along the way? Nothing beats that kind of communication.

I made chicken noodle soup for dinner tonight; feeling like a soup for dinner kind of week. I put on a soft and fuzzy sweater and enjoyed my soup on the couch with a good movie and a nice blanket. I refuse to put the heat on, it's really not that cold out anyway.

Speaking of bills, rent is due November first; finally paying that now that I've got an income. It feels good, I feel more responsible. Probably won't be saying that when it leaves my bank account, but it's the principle that matters. I'm very blessed to be able to live where I am and have the little expenses that I have. Despite all the new things I needed to furnish this place with and my summer expenses, I still have a decent chunk of change left in my savings account. It's nice to be able to replenish it now.

TUESDAY OCTOBER 22ND 2013

I DEBATED ON TACO SOUP OR CHILI FOR DINNER, SO I DECIDED TO MAKE taco soup for taco Tuesday, and I'll make chili on Sunday.

Austin asked Chloe out on a date last night and she said yes. He was so happy this morning, it was nice to see—he looks good happy. He and I talked about where they should have their first date and it was cute watching him act so nervous about the whole thing; it's a different side of him I haven't seen before. He's always been so smooth around me, at least for the most part. He must really be into her.

He decided to take her out to dinner and maybe some bowling after. He doesn't want to take her to a movie yet because he wants to be able to talk with her and get to know her better; I thought that was sweet. I suggested he take her to the Japanese place he took me to, but he just grinned at me and said he'd think about it.

We moved along with the conversation and got back to work. I had a fairly busy day but managed to wrap up around three, three thirty. Sometimes it's a nice break to be caught up on work and waiting on others.

I didn't go to yoga this morning; I wasn't feeling up to getting out of bed to make the extra effort. I hate my period sometimes; it makes me feel so lazy and unmotivated. It also sucks not being able to have sex for a few days. Yeah, I mean Hunter and I don't have sex every time we see each other, but sometimes the mood strikes, and the situation would be much more exciting with sex behind it. Technically, I can skip a period with the birth control pills I'm on, but it can cause more harm than excitement, so I'm not going to mess with it unless I absolutely need to.

Hunter was busy with his studies, so as much as I wanted to send him a picture of my boobs, I decided not to bother him. There's another bonfire on the beach Friday night, so I can tease him then.

I've got the TV muted so I can listen to the wind and thunder roaring outside. It's also forty-three degrees out so I caved and put the heat on low. It's a little too chilly out tonight for my taste.

Granted, it's warmer here than what I would be dealing with back home; I pay bills now so if I want to use the thermostat, I'm going to use the thermostat.

Entry #90

WEDNESDAY OCTOBER 23RD 2013

I HAD DINNER WITH THE PARENTS TONIGHT. DAD MADE CHICKEN, SHRIMP, and some scalloped potatoes with broccoli.

Mom had to work late, so by the time he and I were sitting down, she was just walking in a little after seven.

She had a company meeting with some of the other branch managers from different locations and they're going to cut down on people's hours, starting November first for those working in operations. I wasn't too bummed, but some other people may be. It's better than being laid off in my opinion. Mom felt the same and that's why the meeting ran so late, because she had to figure out how to not lay anyone off. We're not struggling, but we're not operating at our normal, so that's something she has to consider now that she's operating the financials of an entire branch.

Back to dinner plans. Dad wanted to get together for dinner as a family because he misses me and feels like we've all been so busy we haven't been able to spend any time together lately. He's been busy working on this new project for work that he just finished yesterday, so he's excited to be able to relax now.

Mom, well, we know what's going on with her right now.

As for me, it's been nearly two months and they still don't know the truth about Hunter. Not for any specific reason, I'm just enjoying privacy and not having to always explain myself while living under their roof. Yes, now granted I technically still am under their roof, but we're divided by walls, and I pay them rent, so I am my own entity, so to speak.

I told them all was well and that was pretty much that. Mom asked for more details on what I thought about the training from last week and so I told her. She laughed at the information overload comment as she welcomed me into the industry. So, yeah.

I went home to read a book, up until I had a desire to write in here. While I enjoy writing very much, sometimes it can be a real pain in the ass when I'm not in the mood for it. Sometimes when I'm writing I just spit out words that appear in my head, and I don't even know what it is that I've said until I go back and reread it. Sometimes that opens me up to learn new things about myself that I probably otherwise wouldn't say out loud.

Entry #91

DUDE. WE GOT SO STONED OFF THOSE EDIBLES HUNTER MADE LAST NIGHT. I thought I was going to be able to write when I got home, but we passed the fuck out.

Before he left for work, Hunter made us burgers so we could have some dinner in us before taking edibles. Turns out even the meal wouldn't save us because they came out a little too strong.

Don't worry, we instructed the others to take less of a dose than he and I did.

We eventually sobered up enough to where Hunter felt comfortable driving us to the bonfire. We got there a little later than expected, but we didn't care and no one else really noticed.

At one point he and I snuck away and had sex in his jeep; it added to the mood, having to sneak around and be quiet.

Hunter made out with my neck, leaving a big ole hickey behind, before I rode him in the front seat; thankfully he had a condom nearby because raw sex and edibles do not equate to successfully pulling out. Plus, he had a killer grip of my ass, which made for a much more intense fuck.

Stoned quickies are so hot. And the thrill of getting caught only made us want each other more.

When we returned to the fire pit, everyone thought we had left. After they caught on to our escapade, I had absolutely no poker face and the hickey on my neck didn't help us either. Hunter smirked but didn't say a word. Eventually we left and shortly after making it home, I passed out the moment my head hit the pillow.

Currently it's now a little after nine and he's still asleep next to me. I'm going to go take a shower to help get my ass into gear for the day.

◆ ◆ ◆

He woke up and joined me in the shower, then made us some coffee after while I blow-dried my hair.

We were craving lunch instead of breakfast, so we took our time getting ourselves together to go out. He rolled us a joint and we passed it back and forth as we both laid naked in my bed. We eventually made our way out and went to a Mexican place for lunch; chips and salsa hit the spot every time.

Hunter wasn't in the mood to go to work tonight so he swapped shifts with someone and instead has to work tomorrow night, which means he's pulling a double. Totally sucks but he didn't mind too much if it meant he got to relax today.

On the way home, we stopped by his place so he could quickly change and grab some clothes to spend the night again. It seems to be our routine now. I stayed in the jeep and scrolled around on my phone while he grabbed his things.

So, we're not official on social media yet. I mean it's not a huge deal, it is nice keeping my new life down here private, but at the same time it would be cool to have it known that I'm his girl. We are friends on social media though and both of us have our relationship status hidden, so at least we think alike.

I thought about mentioning it to him when he got back, but then I remembered the parents aren't aware yet and if I post it for the world to see, word will get back to them and then they'll wonder why I haven't told them yet.

Ughhhh.

Better keep this to myself for a little bit longer then, I guess.

We went back to my place and spent the day together on the couch watching horror movies. I'm starting to believe those are his favorite.

We were still pretty full from lunch, so we ended up having a late dinner; around like eight is when we finally decided to figure something out. We had a Hawaiian and a buffalo chicken pizza delivered with a side of wings.

I was in the bathroom washing my face, getting ready for bed, when the power suddenly went out. After watching spooky movies all day, you could say I was a little on edge. I'm also not a fan of the dark and my phone was on my nightstand, so I was fuucked.

I was on the verge of a panic attack when Hunter knocked on the door to save me from the dark. We then walked around my place and gathered all my candles so we could have some kind of light.

Mental note to buy flashlights please.

The parents texted to see if I was okay; they lost power too. It's thirty degrees outside and we have no power or heat now. The electric company said it'll be a few hours before it's back on...

Hunter and I decided to make the most of it, so we set the scene and cozied up together under the covers, passing a joint back and forth to help pass the time. Conversation was flowing well until the mood suddenly changed when Hunter said he had something he wanted to tell me. My heart sank into my chest, not knowing what he was about to confess. He switched positions and was now sitting up and leaning against the headboard. It seemed serious.

He assured me that he didn't mean to hide this from me, he just wasn't ready to share it with me yet. I grew more nervous but continued to listen.

He explained that his parents passed away when he was little, so he was raised by his grandparents.

He then told me about his older sister that is married and living in Georgia, so he has no other family besides her and his uncle.

My heart sank, I felt horrible for him. The more he spoke about his family, the more I understood why he waited to tell me. He went on to mention that since his grandparents have passed, the holidays tend to be a little harder for him, and if he seems a little off these next few months, he wanted me to know why. Apparently, his sister is so busy with her career and family, they don't see each other very often. Granted they talk every week; it's been almost two years since they've actually seen each other in person.

As far as his uncle goes, they see each other almost every day at work so they have a solid relationship. They usually spend most of the holidays together when he's not with his sister.

I heard the loneliness behind his voice, I felt so bad.

It then brought up the conversation where he talked about what he hopes his future will look like someday. After his career has taken off, he wants two or three kids, a house with a pool and a deck, a garage so he can work in it, and a dog or two.

I've always wanted a dog, but the parents would never allow it. It's good to know he's a dog person.

While he was reminiscing on what he wants for his future, he paused to look at me, then stopped. He seemed panicked for a second and told me he hoped that didn't scare me away.

Little did he know I was fantasizing right along there with him.

I told him he was fine and that I agreed, however I wanted two or three dogs since I wasn't allowed to have any pets growing up. He looked at me, smiled, and said, "Two or three dogs it is then."

My brain melted.

Did he just sneak in a comment about a future together? It's so soon though, we've only known each other for four months. Though does time really matter when you think you've met the one?

The vibe in the room changed when we realized we had just unintentionally pictured a future together.

He pulled me over and I straddled him. He kissed me, I kissed him, next thing you know we're fooling around in the dark by candlelight. It smelled like a mixture of salty oceans with a hint of vanilla bean, with a soft amber glow beaming off each other's skin. Probably one of the most romantic settings I've ever been in despite the cold.

I'm not sure what came over us, but it was probably our most passionate make out session to date. It was electrifying… every time our lips touched, the excitement throughout our bodies intensified. Dude, the second he pushed himself inside of me, I could feel my eyes roll to the back of my head. Maybe it has something to do with how cold it is in the room or maybe it's the scenery, I truly don't know, but what we just did together was definitely on a deeper level than sex. I think we just made love for the first time?

Hunter's asleep next to me and my phone is about to die; I've been using the flashlight app so I could see to write. The power company estimates the power to be restored sometime in the middle of the night. Fun times.

Maybe I'm just all up in my feelings, but I think I'm going to be Hunter's wife someday.

Entry #92

SATURDAY NOVEMBER 2ND 2013

HALLOWEEN WAS COOL, PEOPLE DRESSED UP AT WORK, AND I HAD NO trick or treaters, so now I get to spend the next three months eating the candy I bought.

Paying rent yesterday felt so freeing—hopefully this feeling never goes away. I'm extremely thankful I can afford to do it. I know it's not much, but it's something.

Poor Hunter had to work this morning, so he headed out pretty early. Though me on the other hand... I slept in until around eleven and damn was that very much needed. One of his friends threw a Halloween party last night, but he and I never made it. He came to pick me up and once he saw me, well, he had to have me. And quite honestly, I had to have him too.

I should rewind a little so I can shed some light on the situation that was last night.

I'm not the best at planning Halloween costumes, so Hunter had full pick. He chose for us to go as undercover spies. I had no idea of any party plans; I just needed to know the attire and what time he was picking me up. I kind of dig when he tells me what to do, but I can't let him know that yet, at least not until after there's a ring on my finger.

BRB I want some breakfast.

• • •

Don't hate, you write better after you've eaten something.

Anywho. Let me tell you what happened.

When he walked through the front door, you could immediately tell by the look on his face that his thoughts were up to no good. He was wearing black pants and black shoes, a black shirt with the sleeves rolled up, with a black tie. He had a silver watch on his left wrist. His hair was smooth and his beard well groomed… he looked way too sexy to be standing in my front door.

Now as for me, I wore a long, flowy red chiffon dress with a red choker that had a wonderful display of my boobs. It also had a slit down the side so you could catch a glimpse of my leg as I walked by. I paired it with my black heels and shiny, bright cherry-red lipstick. I even leveled up and curled my hair… it's been a very long time since I've done that, but every time I do it bounces beautifully.

If only he knew then what I was wearing underneath my dress.

He walked in just as I was getting ready to put my coat on. Our eyes met and I let out a "fuck me" sigh so loud, he most certainly heard it.

I couldn't help it, I was smitten. Weak in my knees, if you will.

I was frozen in my tracks and locked in on his emerald-green eyes as he slowly made his way over to me. I was so mesmerized by his appearance and that fancy French cologne of his that I couldn't form any sentences. He towered over me and asked if I wanted to take a shot of whiskey with him—didn't mention anything about the party, nor did he take his eyes off me once.

He pulled out two glasses and put four ice cubes in each, pouring just enough whiskey to coat the ice and then some. Then he walked back over to me and told me we weren't going to the party anymore because he wouldn't be able to keep his hands off of me looking the way I do.

I smiled and replied, "Yes, Daddy." His eyes grew wide and his smile wider. We tapped our glasses and took our shot.

He unlocked a boyfriend perk that night. Quite a few actually, but I'll get to that.

He had me bring him his ear buds, one for him and one for me. While he put a playlist together, I lit some candles and turned the lights off in hopes of recreating the romantic glow from the other night.

I returned to find him still leaning against the counter choosing the songs he wanted us to listen to.

I decided to be ballsy.

I carefully took his phone out of his hands, set it down on the counter, and pressed play to whatever was left on the screen. The volume was low enough for us to talk, but it created the perfect background to this moment we were creating.

I grabbed his tie and slid it through my hands, almost like I was feeling him up. The eye contact was strong; we sized each other up and down with our hungry eyes.

I unbuttoned his shirt as he loosened his tie. He brushed my hair off my right shoulder, so I ran my fingers through to fluff it up a little. He really likes the curls by the way (take note).

I kissed him on his cheek and slowly moved down the side of his neck; I stopped at his chest.

He unzipped my dress and discovered what I had on underneath… a pink lace garter lingerie set. I was still in my heels, so I was only at a slightly higher level than usual.

I was heavily influenced by his scent and the moment we were in, so I kept up with leading the way. I slid down his pants, got on my knees, and gave him head. By the time I was done with him, my cherry-red lipstick was all over him.

We backed up over to the kitchen table and he lowered me onto my back. I barely understood how to get in this garter set, let alone how to get out of it, so he slid my underwear to the side and ate me out like the bad ass sexy spy that he was. The background music really added to the suspense, he chose a killer playlist.

We moved to my bedroom and undressed a little more. He used his tie to tie my wrists behind my back before bending me over and finishing me off from behind. He even reached around the front to rub my pussy a bit. That was a nice surprise. After we finished and were back in the kitchen sipping on more whiskey, he mentioned that he likes it when I call him Daddy.

Food started to sound like a good idea, so we ordered from an Italian place and spent the rest of the night on the couch together drinking whiskey, eating pasta, and watching movies. We were very drunk by the time we made it to bed. Pasta only soaked up so much alcohol.

We sixty-nined right before bed. It was a little challenging because we were drunk and feeling a little bubbly, but we made it work.

I swear, every time Hunter tells me he loves me, it makes me feel like the luckiest girl in the world. I still can't believe we found each other.

Who knew I was going to find love so shortly after moving here... and to think I was first rejecting the idea. I mean yeah, I wanted to figure some things out for myself and I'm very thankful that I did. It's just crazy to think about how what's been in front of me all this time is what's been right for me all along. I'm just really thankful that we found each other.

Speaking of Hunter. He just texted me that he's thinking about my red dress from last night and hopes to see me in it again. He's working a double today and a double tomorrow... last night was the first time we have seen each other all week. He's been busy with school, and I've been wrapped in my work. We've been video chatting here and there, which is a new thing I'm enjoying doing with him.

The weather has cooled down a good bit but there are some warm days sneaking in between, here and there. There's a bonfire planned for next Friday night on the beach that I'm really looking forward to. I'm going to wear my suspender skirt with a green undershirt and a beanie to match, weather permitting of course. I'm excited.

Entry # 93

WE GAINED AN HOUR TODAY. I LOVE/HATE THIS TIME OF YEAR.

I legitimately did nothing but lounge in bed and on the couch yesterday. It was fantastic, though I was feeling a little lazy today, so I cleaned the house and did some food shopping. Smoked a joint when I got home while I put everything away and prepped lunch for the week. I made General Tso's flavored chicken with rice noodles and sliced zucchini… it smelled so good, I wanted it right then and there, but I was having dinner with the parents since I missed breakfast with them this morning.

They want to talk Thanksgiving plans… The bulk of the family is supposedly wanting to come down and visit, so we'll see how this conversation goes tonight.

Hazel called me to see what I was up to and to brag about the Halloween party Max and his brother threw on Friday night. Made me wonder if that was the party Hunter was taking me to, but there's no way that's possible because Hunter and Max don't know each other. I've never heard Max's name mentioned by Hunter, or anyone else we've hung out with.

Could you fucking imagine if Hunter and Max knew each other? Deep down, Hunter was the one I always wanted, but that doesn't mean I didn't have fun when I was spending time with Max.

Yo, could you imagine if Max, Hunter, AND Austin all knew each other?

I'm high, I need to calm down. This is too much to be thinking about right now, and I really don't need to be stressing myself over a scenario my anxiety is creating in my head.

Hazel was still talking as I was in my head thinking, so while I felt kind of bad, she didn't seem to notice so there was no harm there. From the bits and pieces I heard, it sounded like an incredible night. But nothing beats role-playing in sexy outfits with your boyfriend, getting drunk, and fooling around all night. I'd take a night like that over a party anytime.

She finally asked about my night and so I told her; held back some details just because, but gave her the highlights and that was pretty much it. Gossiping with friends about sex is probably one of the best conversations you could have. You can learn so much.

We rambled on for about an hour and then I realized it was dinnertime. I was still coming down from my high, but I wasn't as paranoid as I was earlier, so that was nice. We hung up and I went next door for dinner. They made an oven stuffer, roasted sweet potatoes, salad, and broccoli.

Regarding Thanksgiving, just about EVERYONE is coming. On Mom's side: her sister, brother-in-law, and the cousins. Dad's: his parents and his brother. That's what, seven people, plus me, the parents, and Hunter?

I still haven't told them about him. I'm sure they suspect something, but they haven't asked so I haven't brought it up.

Why haven't I told them yet?

On the positive side to all these visitors, none of them are staying with me. They're all getting hotel rooms or staying with the parents, so I'm safe. This Thanksgiving is going to be interesting all right.

When dinner was over, I helped clean up and went home. Hunter called me as he was getting ready to leave and I told him what my family wanted to do. When I asked him what he wanted to do, he had some big plans of his own.

He wanted to see how I felt about doing a Friendsgiving at his place with his roommate, Scarlett's brother, me of course, and anyone else I wanted to invite. I thought of Scarlett and Hazel, so I mentioned it and he said that would be awesome. I confessed that I hadn't told the parents about us yet, so I had to figure out a way to navigate that day. He didn't seem to mind, but he didn't really respond to it either. I told him I would figure it out and all he said was, "That sounds good."

Yikes... Does his family know about me? I honestly have no idea, we haven't talked about it.

Entry #94

I CALLED SCARLETT ON MY WAY TO THE OFFICE AND TOLD HER ABOUT Thanksgiving plans. She asked if she could bring a guest and I told her yes, though she failed to mention who it was, just that they and her brother would all drive down together. I was curious but didn't push. We were too excited and gushing over our plans for me to worry.

She asked me if I told the parents about Hunter yet, and when I told her no, she had that same tone Hunter did when I told him. I asked her what the deal was, and she told me it's been long enough and that I probably should so Hunter doesn't feel like I'm hiding him or something. I thought that was a bit dramatic, but then again, I wonder if she could be right?

I told her I would introduce him at Thanksgiving; this way we can say hi to the family for a little bit then leave. A quick in and out so it's not so overwhelming meeting so many new people at once.

Work was a little slow. We have a few loans in processing, but not the typical. To be fair, they say it slows down this time of year naturally, so we'll see how things go.

Austin has been keeping his distance at work. Not just from me but from everyone. He's studying for his LO test and apparently, it's not an easy exam. The passing rate is about 58% and it's designed to trick you. He's been kept up in his space for about a month now. According to

Mom, he's taking his test right before Thanksgiving, so he's taking advantage of the downtime during the day for some extra studying. Seems intense. Once he's done, I'll have to pick his brain about it sometime.

I called Hunter on my way home from yoga and we talked about Thanksgiving. I asked him if he would like to meet my family and he sounded excited. I told him we would say hi for a little while then head out so we could prep for his event. He was down for that. I told him Scarlett was coming with a plus one, along with her brother. So, them plus his roommate and me equals six of us. Not a bad group of people.

Hazel is going to meet Max's brother's family for Thanksgiving. She's finally meeting his parents; she's hella nervous but mostly excited. I think she'll be just fine.

Hunter asked for my input on the menu and basically told me that he'll make me anything I desire.

I told him we could talk about it when we see each other Friday night. He's got a lot of upcoming exams that he needs to focus on before the holiday break, so we're giving each other some space. It sucks because we live so close together and it's tempting to want to sneak over, but I respect what he's doing and don't want to distract him. He gave me space to be me during the summer, so he deserves that same respect. At least we still make time to talk to each other when we can, that's what's most important. My lunch tasted amazing today, by the way; so glad I found this new sauce to cook with. It was a garlic sauce that I poured over some chicken and threw over a bed of lettuce with some sliced grape tomatoes.

Entry #95

THURSDAY NOVEMBER 7ᵀᴴ 2013

NAVIGATING THIS DAY WITHOUT BEING ABLE TO TALK ABOUT WHAT I DREAMT of last night was horrible. I had a nightmare about my car accident. I relived the entire thing, only in my dream I died.

Mom wasn't in the office and there wasn't a whole lot of work to focus on, so I texted back and forth with Hazel and Scarlett, trying to pretend I didn't dream that I died in an accident I barely survived in real life.

I haven't thought about it in so long, so why now?

Hunter called me after he got off class and was heading home to eat dinner and study. He could tell something was off and I brushed it off by saying I had a bad dream. Well, for whatever reason, Hunter won't let me be down in my feelings, so I finally told him that I had something from my past that I haven't talked about with him yet.

We stayed on the phone until we both got to my place; he ordered Chinese for dinner, and we talked on the couch. I told him everything.

I started by explaining how I was able to afford to take the summer off. While the parents covered the moving expenses, I have technically been on my own since we got here. When I got to the actual car accident part, I told him how I was hit by a drunk driver who was speeding and ran a red light.

He hugged me so tightly, I didn't want him to ever let go.

I felt like I needed to share the details so I could shake my dream, so I explained how the driver hit me straight into the driver's side of my car. I started to get emotional when I told him how the driver was only six inches away from killing me head on.

I went on to explain how I later woke up in a hospital room with the parents by my side talking to the surgeon. How they were both in tears, petrified, just holding each other as they listened intently to the recovery journey I had ahead of me. I had three broken ribs which punctured a lung, cuts all over my arms, face, and legs. I had severe whiplash, a broken shoulder, and my rotator cuff was torn so badly, I needed surgery to repair it. I was initially told I had three to six months of recovery and physical therapy ahead of me… but it turned into nearly twelve months instead.

I went on about how the car accident also flipped a switch on my immune system, and I developed an autoimmune disease called Fibromyalgia. I grew more emotional when I told him that's why I try really hard to keep my body moving and as healthy as I possibly can. Why I was so incredibly thankful to have been given the opportunity to move down here, because honestly, staying in New York was killing me on the inside. I just never knew what the issue was until I got away from it.

I LAID IT ALL OUT ON THE TABLE. Even brought up some feelings I didn't realize I was feeling. I have not once ever told anyone about the misery I was feeling back home. Couldn't believe I was saying it out loud; this goes to show how comfortable I am with him.

While it wasn't an easy conversation, I do feel relieved now that he knows. He appreciated me opening up and now I think he gets me a little better.

He asked if anyone else here knew and I told him no. He didn't ask why but I felt inclined to tell him anyway. He understood not wanting to be the center of people's attention (and gossip), considering his parents died when he was younger.

We moved onto something more positive when dinner finally arrived. We ate and had a TV show playing in the background. Time went on and it got late. Hunter's got an exam in the morning, and I had felt guilty enough for dumping this on him how and when I did, so we called it a night and here you find me.

I'm glad that I finally told Hunter about what happened. Our pasts are finally all laid out on the table.

It's crazy how I dreamt of that last night when it's been so long since it happened. Even crazier how I finally put it out there how unhappy I was back home. I mean sure, I had some friends and did some things, but now that I'm no longer there, it's as if I never even existed in the first place. Everyone has moved on, of course including me, but that doesn't mean it still doesn't hurt a little sometimes.

Do I wish I still lived back home? Not in any way, shape, or form.

Do I have positive memories that I miss from time to time? Well, yes, and that's okay. I guess New York was a stepping stone for me. It's who I was, but no longer who I am.

Now I'm someone who does what I want simply because it makes me happy. I wear the clothes I want to wear and spend my days how I want to be spending them. I now choose who I give my all to instead of doing so out of obligation.

Entry #96

IT WAS CHILLIER THAN I EXPECTED, SO I HAD TO WEAR A HOODIE WITH MY suspender skirt because the outfit was too good not to be seen in, especially for a sexy bonfire beach night. Hunter wore jeans, a T-shirt, and a beanie. The winter look is a very good look on him and he hasn't shaven his face in a few days, so he's got a sexy stubble going on.

I was so hot for him on the ride over, I thought I was going to melt in my seat. Yeah, part of it is him being older than me and more experienced with life, but the other part is the way he carries himself. He knows who he is, and he is not afraid to go after what he wants. Something about that appetite of his just really gets me going.

Back to the bonfire.

Hazel was there with Max's brother and she and I talked about the upcoming holidays while the guys talked about sports.

It's football season so they've got a lot to argue about right now. The masculinity this time of year in the South is pretty high. They even tend to go apeshit over college games down here, so let's just say football is on most people's brains this time of year.

Hunter works the night shift tomorrow, so he was able to enjoy himself tonight. He had a hell of a week, so I told him I would drive us home. Considering my confession to him last night, he was a little hesitant, but I convinced him to chill and relax. He had a few beers, I smoked with Hazel, and the rest of the girls chugged some wine. I secretly wanted to, but I already told Hunter he could drink and I like how loose he gets when he's relaxed, so I took one for the team and sat this one out.

We headed out a little after eleven and grabbed some food on the way back to my place. We ate on the couch and watched a movie until we were ready to be more comfortable in bed.

Hunter and I were vibing on two different levels. He was totally into himself, where I was feeling a little shy. Quick on my feet, I said we should take advantage and role-play like it was my first time with a guy. He couldn't have moved over to me fast enough.

We were both now sitting on the edge of the bed fully dressed, bodies facing front, but heads turned to face each other. I don't remember what he said but he just started making this casual small talk with me and he really eased his way into a conversation; it was so damn sexy the way he just took control. Wasn't long until he asked if he could kiss me, I blushed faster than I could say yes.

We leaned in to kiss and my heart was pounding so fast he must have heard it.

So, we're making out and his hands are around my waist. I don't like being teased for too long, so I fixed that and accelerated to second base. He stopped kissing me, looked me in my eyes, and was like, "You don't seem so shy to me." To which I replied, "Sorry, Daddy, my curiosity got the best of me."

I totally fucking won that evening ha-ha.

Next I knew, we were naked and he was on top of me covering every inch of my body with his lips. He spread my legs apart and kissed the inside of my thighs, slowly moving from the left side, over to the right, all the way up and over my torso, until he landed on my lips. In between kissing me he told me what he was going to do to me next. Then he slowly inserted his fingers inside me… Two in the pink and one for the clit is all that needs to be said for me to read back on this someday and remember how good it felt.

When he asked me if I was ready for him to be inside me, I told him yes. He pulled out of me and sucked on his fingers to taste me.

He teased me with the tip before slowly sliding inside me, and he did this thing where he would go back and forth, pulling out and pushing himself in, and it fucking drove me nuts.

He finally railed into me when I told him I couldn't take it anymore and to "just give it to me." He laughed, switched gears, and said, "Yes ma'am." If we weren't having sex at the time, I would have given him shit for calling me that. But if I'm being brutally honest here, that Southern drawl of his makes just about anything sound sexy.

Entry # 97

SCARLETT STILL WON'T TELL ME WHO HER THANKSGIVING PLUS ONE IS and it's driving me nuts. I'm not really sure why it's bothering me so much, I guess I just don't understand the secrecy.

Is that who we are to each other now?

Mom assigned me a task to redesign the company's website, so guess who is now writing posts for our new blog! I have no idea what I am going to write about yet, but I'm excited for the opportunity. A little nervous to be so open with my writing for the first time, but more excited for the possibilities ahead.

It's been cold and rainy these past few days and it's been very frustrating because nobody down here knows how to drive when it rains, and now that it gets dark out earlier, it's even worse.

Hunter has worked every night after school this week to pick up some extra shifts so he can spend his time off from school relaxing. I totally understand his thinking for that, I just don't want him to burn himself out. He currently seems to be doing well, so I hope it continues.

Max's brother had to work tonight so Hazel came by, and she and I ordered food and drank a bunch of wine. We were challenged with finding the perfect wine for her to bring for when she meets her boyfriend's parents, so of course we had to try a few different kinds to find the best one. We legit had six bottles of wine between the two of us, it was insane.

At one point she video chatted with Max's brother, so I took that time to throw on some comfy clothes, wash my face, and check in with Hunter. He called me while he was on his way home, and he laughed at how drunk I was. He wanted in on the fun, but Hazel was spending the night, so he went home and gamed, and we spent the night texting while Hazel and I watched movies and ate snacks.

She's currently passed out on the couch right now and I'm in bed. I can't sleep, which is why you find me here. I might just put a movie on and try to fall asleep. I have a feeling this is going to feel pretty rough in the morning.

Entry #98

SATURDAY NOVEMBER 16TH 2013

TALK ABOUT A FUCKING HANGOVER FROM HELL. HAZEL AND I WOKE UP A little after twelve, practically lunchtime, both dizzy and weak as can be. I had a text from Hunter not to worry about lunch because he had a feeling we would need some food, so he ordered us some burgers, wings, and fries that were delivered within an hour of Hazel and I waking up. It was the sweetest thing and perfectly well timed.

What a man...

Eventually Hazel left and went home. I dragged my ass into the tub, thinking I could sweat out any remaining alcohol from my system. Lasted about ten minutes before I was hot and bothered, so I took a cool shower and laid in bed until Hunter told me he was off work and heading over this way.

It was a little too chilly out for mini golf, so we decided to go bowling instead. My hangover was feeling a little better, but the constant bending down mini golf requires would not have been fun for me.

We spent about two hours bowling a few games and munching on some of the good ole bowling alley food. Enjoyed a few drinks together and really just took our time hanging out. Hunter is a way better bowler than I am, but with practice I could probably get to his level. Maybe.

Entry #99

FRIDAY NOVEMBER 22ND 2013

I REALLY HATE BEING ON MY PERIOD SOMETIMES.

Well, I always do, but some months are just a little more difficult than others. This week has been filled with emotional ups and downs I really was not trying to experience given how busy the week started off with work. Thankfully, towards the end it slowed down, but damn, Monday and Tuesday were just exhausting. With the holiday break next week, everyone is a little on edge about making sure everything is done as it should be.

Luckily for me, I managed to create some blog posts I've now got scheduled for the next month, so that's a positive step in the right direction.

Hunter finished his new story mode on this game that he wanted to beat, and Scarlett and I have been talking on the phone all week about Thanksgiving. Went over outfit choices, menu items, and all the things. Thankfully, Hunter and I figured out our menu already, so now we just have to scramble around to get all the things from the store. I decided to stop asking about her plus one because clearly, she isn't going to tell me.

Austin passed his LO test, so Mom took the whole office out for a round of drinks today after work to celebrate. Something we all haven't done in a while, so it was fun to get together. I know I don't talk about or associate myself with the other coworkers much, but they're cool people. Austin and I are the youngest, which is why we get along so well.

. . .

Oh hey. Sooooo long story short, Hunter and I got into our first tiff.

All is well and he and I are totally fine, he's in the kitchen right now grabbing us some water and snacks while I finish this up before we put on a movie. He's working a double tomorrow and Sunday so he can take off all next week.

Anyway, Chloe met us at the bar to celebrate with Austin and she and I drank a little too much while getting to know each other. *She's actually super cool by the way, I can see why she and Austin click.*

Well, instead of calling Hunter for a ride home, I chose to accept Chloe's offer for Austin to drive me home with them. I really didn't think anything of it, but now after talking with Hunter I can understand where he is coming from.

He's not mad, he was just a little upset that I was in trouble (too drunk to drive) and didn't call him—he just wants to be the man who rescues me when I need help, is all. It's not that I didn't think about calling him, I just didn't want to bother him. But I guess that's the old version of me talking, because while I can take care of myself, I have a man in my life now and if he wants to help me then I should give him the opportunity to do just that.

Entry #100

ONE-HUNDRED ENTRIES. HOLY MOLY, MY FRIEND, THIS JOURNAL IS GETTING serious.

Hunter left early yesterday morning, and after he left, I couldn't fall back to sleep, so I spent the day deep cleaning the house, getting it ready for Thanksgiving. Scarlett said she got a hotel room for her and her plus one, so she doesn't need to crash here, so that means she is 100% bringing a date. Which is fine, but like who the fuck is it?

Sunday morning breakfast was… intense, but overall, it went well. I finally told the parents about Hunter and explained that I would not be staying for Thanksgiving because I will be with him. Mom was not entirely thrilled given who all was coming, but she calmed down a little when I told her I could help with anything she needed in the morning and that Hunter would be stopping by to say hello and meet everyone. Dad was just relieved to finally learn about the jeep that he's seen in front of the house for the last few months. Overall, both are happy for me and excited to meet the Southerner who stole my Northern heart.

After breakfast, Mom and I ironed out some Thanksgiving details before going our separate ways. She was cool with me riding with her to work tomorrow, but I think she was punishing me because I have to be ready much earlier; she needs to be at the office by eight tomorrow and I don't roll in until nine, so that'll be fun. I'm used to being awake that early, so it wasn't the end of the world, it's more so the thought of getting to work an hour earlier that doesn't sound appealing. I thought about asking Hunter for a ride, but I know how excited he is to finally sleep in.

As for today, I spent the day being lazy, binge watching this new medical drama show I've recently started. Since my period is finally over, I snuck in a little time with my bullet and fucked myself on the couch—it was pretty sweet, it's been a hot minute since I've played with myself.

$\mathcal{E}ntry$ #101

MONDAY NOVEMBER 25TH 2013

THE RIDE TO WORK WITH MOM WASN'T SO BAD, SHE TREATED US TO COFfee and breakfast that we grabbed on the way in. That was a nice way to start the day.

She asked about Hunter and all these different things about him, and so I told her a few things without giving her all the details. She knows we started off as friends and how he knows Scarlett's brother. Told her all about Friendsgiving plans and she was really excited for me. I know she's bummed I won't be around all day with her and the family, but I know she's fine with it because it's not like I won't be around at all, so it'll be fine.

On the flipside, the office is closed Wednesday, Thursday, and Friday of this week, so that'll be a nice mini vacay.

Hunter slept in and when he texted me, he mentioned he was craving Chinese, so I thought it would be nice to send some food and return the favor. This way he could enjoy his day until it's time for dinner, since he wants to cook for us tonight.

Work was very slow, so we got to leave at two. I did another hot yoga class and this time I wore shorts so I didn't totally die of heat exhaustion.

As I was passing by to leave, Chloe was walking in and she stopped me for a minute and asked for my number. She mentioned she had a great time hanging out and getting to know me on Friday and wanted to see if I would want to be friends. Considering my confusing, lust-filled past with Austin, I was a little conflicted as to whether I should or not, but like, all Austin and I ever did was kiss. Maybe if we slept together, I would dodge my way out of it, but instead I decided to go along with it, and so I gave her my number.

Immediately wondered if I should have cleared that with Austin first? Eh, maybe I'll tell him tomorrow, so he knows. I just don't want anything to be awkward.

• • •

Just got back from Hunter's. He made salmon for dinner, and it tasted amazing. He tried this new smokey flavor and it worked out perfectly. Didn't feel like watching a movie, so we ran to the grocery store after dinner so we could knock out our Friendsgiving shopping list together. For a quick shopping trip, we had a great time goofing off in the store together. I pushed the cart while he walked behind and pushed with me, whispering dirty things in my ear when he wasn't throwing things in the cart like the bad ass chef he is. He wouldn't even let me pay for any of the groceries; he insisted, but I also insisted, so he gave in and let me handle the alcohol and desserts.

He's so sweet, I fucking love him.

I love us.

Entry #102

YOO WORK DRAGGED ASS TODAY. LUCKILY, WE GOT OFF AT TWO AGAIN.

Austin didn't come into the office, so I'll have to tell him about Chloe another time. Unless she tells him, but either way I need to be clear with him so no wires get crossed.

I don't need it slipping that he and I have been wrapped up in each other's arms before.

Hunter gamed all day and missed lunch, I too had missed lunch, so he told me to swing by after yoga and he'd make us some dinner. I didn't want to show up to his place all sweaty, so I raced home to change and shower before meeting him.

He made cauliflower crusted flatbread pizzas: pepperoni, supreme, and margherita flavored. Oh man were they cooked perfectly; they had the best crunch, and oil dripped down the side of my hands just like the pizza did back home.

I was so hungry, and the pizza was so good, I totally just ate in front of him like I didn't even care if he was watching me or not.

Come to think about it, before the car accident I never finished my food in front of people. I would take the leftovers home with me or save them for later when I could be alone. I guess I was just worried about people associating me as the heavy girl who liked to eat.

Keep going...

In all honesty, so much has changed because of the car accident. The parents and I developed a stronger relationship. Now granted, I had no choice because I needed a lot of help, but it did open us up to a deeper level of communication that really helped me get myself to where I am today. If it wasn't for them refusing to give up on me, who knows, I may have given up on myself.

Hunter has introduced me to new friendships, new experiences, and a new perspective on life. Somehow, he now has managed to get me to feel comfortable eating in front of someone for the first time since I can honestly remember. I may have grown up with body image issues that I continue to struggle with from time to time, but I can happily say that I have, for the most part, left most of those feelings behind.

Previously, everyone around me constantly complained about their weight and how they looked, so I thought that was the norm. Now that I'm in a new environment and away from it, I know that's not how you're supposed to live. Breaking free of my insecurities has been a tough battle, but I'm getting stronger every single day.

Moving to South Carolina really helped me rid myself of a lot more baggage than I initially thought. I guess it is true—time and new places really can heal all wounds.

Entry #103

I STAYED AT HUNTER'S UNTIL MIDNIGHT LAST NIGHT. HE TOLD ME I COULD have spent the night, but I really just wanted to be in my own bed. It's the week of a major holiday. Clearly, I have a lot to write about.

The family gets in tonight and the parents are making me have dinner over there so I can see everyone before tomorrow. I mean, to be fair they aren't exactly "making me," but it was strongly encouraged, so I'll be going over there for dinner tonight after everyone gets in and settled. Well, everyone on Mom's side; Dad's will all be here tomorrow morning.

• • •

Mom made her famous lasagna and stuffed shells for dinner, with some salad and garlic bread. It was amazing and I totally took home some leftovers. Why she took it upon herself to cook such a filling meal the day before Thanksgiving, I will never understand, but she did an amazing job.

It was nice to show the family around the new house, and even more so, my new place. Of course, we had the daunting "what's new" conversation during dinner, and when it got to be my turn, I wasn't sure what to say, so I kept it short and sweet. The cousins' eyebrows perked when I mentioned Hunter, but I'm not going to worry about it for now.

Speaking of, he and I have been texting back and forth all night; he's heading this way in a few minutes so we can spend the night together. Almost thought about introducing him to my cousins tonight, but it can wait for tomorrow. I do love my family but damn they can be so motherfucking nosey sometimes.

Entry #104

THURSDAY NOVEMBER 28ᵀᴴ 2013

HUNTER'S IN THE SHOWER RIGHT NOW. I'M STALLING GETTING MYSELF together because I'm a little nervous to introduce him to the family. Maybe if I told the parents about him sooner, it wouldn't be so over-whelming introducing him to everyone at once, but maybe with every-one being distracted by holiday things, it'll take the pressure off a little. He sure doesn't seem nervous at all… he seems excited, and seeing him excited to meet my family makes me happy.

Scarlett, her plus one, and her brother are arriving closer to two, so we have some time to do the things we need to do.

Fuck, I'm so nervous.

He just turned the shower off and I'm not even dressed. Wish me luck. BRB.

. . .

So… a lot has happened, I made it a priority to get back in here. I just, I don't know what to fucking think right now. I'll start from the beginning.

Introducing Hunter to the family went well. When we walked in the door, all the men were glued to the TV, watching football. Mom,

Grandma, and my aunt were in the kitchen cooking. I first introduced Hunter to everyone in the living room, but nobody really seemed to pay attention except Dad. He stood up to meet Hunter, shook his hand for a minute, and that was the end of that. Some rival game was going on with the family's favorite team, so they were all in their feelings about it.

When I brought him into the kitchen, everyone was scrambling doing something, but they all took a minute to say hi and introduce themselves. Mom liked the flowers he brought her and thanked him before making a sarcastic comment about seeing his jeep here all the time.

I could tell she was kidding, but like really, did we have to do this now?

Hunter and I stayed for a little to help prep; he was praised for his chef abilities and that took the attention away from us not staying to eat. Everyone seemed to really like him, and it was nice watching him fit in with everyone. Around noon was when we headed out to his place so we could get into some prepping of our own; thankfully, Hunter's roommate had already gotten a head start on some things.

Now as for the bullshit drama, see for yourself.

Around two o'clock, Scarlett texted they were on the way. They showed up and when they came inside, I did not fucking expect to see Benji with them. Scarlett's brother went straight to the kitchen to meet Hunter in person for the first time ever. Hunter's roommate was in the kitchen with him, so it was just me, Scarlett, and Benji in the living room. I only answered the door because the guys were busy doing something and my hands were free.

Not even a heads up that my best friend was bringing my ex-boyfriend to my current boyfriend's Friendsgiving?! I was fucking besides myself; I had no idea what to think.

I pulled Scarlett to the side so we could talk in private, and I asked her what the fuck was going on. Benji was alone in the living room. She confessed that they had been seeing each other these past couple of months. I demanded an explanation, and she gave me one all right.

She told me a story about how her and Benji worked at the restaurant late one night, alone, and bumped into each other while they were cleaning. It had been a very long day and they just wanted to be done for the night. Apparently, when they bumped into each other, they made instant eye contact that caught Scarlett off guard, so she smiled and blushed. Benji told her she had a beautiful smile and they stared at each other in silence until Benji leaned in and kissed her. Apparently, they were super into it until Scarlett pulled back and mentioned my name. She said she felt bad, so they agreed to keep it between themselves and continued on like nothing had happened. They soon called it a night and headed home separately.

That was a Thursday night and they had to work together again the next day. After cleaning up Friday night, they were alone again and talked; they agreed it was a mistake and to put it on the back burner. Then they worked together all day Saturday... It was one of their busiest days yet, and some people called out, so they scrambled the entire day to keep up with the demands of their customers. Hustling side by side to make sure business would continue to run as smoothly as possible.

By the end of the day, they were pumped from getting through such a challenging day. Scarlett said they locked eyes again and eventually one thing led to another, and they slept together that night. She followed that up with a comment about how they're in love and she wanted to tell me in person.

This was not exactly the most appropriate time for this kind of reveal, and why she felt the need to do this in this way, I will never understand. I'm a little hurt that she surprised me like this on a day like today.

I wasn't mad that they were together, I was angrier at the fact that this was the way she decided to break the news to me.

Hunter called out for me, so I went over to him and introduced Scarlett and Benji as my best friend and ex-lover who are now in love with each other. That shifted the mood in the room, so Scarlett's brother poured some shots and Hunter pulled me into his room for a minute. I got a little emotional and told him how I had no idea who Scarlett was bringing and that I didn't know about any of it and just rambled on about how bad I felt about the whole thing. I clarified to him that I was not jealous and reminded him that I was the one who ended things with Benji.

He wiped the tears off my face, hugged me, and told me it was totally fine and that he wasn't feeling any type of way about it, he was more worried about how I was feeling. He was very sweet and helped calm me down. When we returned to the rest of the crowd, I decided not to let this bother me and went on with the day as best as I could.

Hunter let me do my thing and set the table so I could make it look all fancy-like. He did such an amazing job with all the food; everything was great, and people loved it. We had turkey that he rubbed with a buttery herb, lemon/orange citrus mixture, stuffing, garlic mashed potatoes, green bean casserole, mashed sweet potatoes, mac and cheese, pickles and olives, corn, and roasted brussels sprouts drizzled in olive oil, salt, and pepper, topped with bacon. OMG it was so much food.

Scarlett had the idea for us all to take turns sharing something we were thankful for. I hesitated… thankfully Hunter led the conversation, and everyone chose their words carefully, so it all worked out and wasn't awkward.

After dinner, I told Hunter I'd clean so he could relax for the rest of the evening and enjoy himself. It took a little convincing, but I managed to get him to agree, so he went in the living room with the guys and Scarlett stayed behind to help me clean up. While it was not a great feeling knowing my ex and current boyfriend were in the same room together, I was honestly more anxious to be alone with Scarlett.

As soon as the kitchen cleared, she immediately began apologizing. I told her it didn't really bother me so much that they're together, what hurt more was how she told me. She said she wanted to do it in person and couldn't hide it from me any longer because she felt like she's been lying to me. I get that, but like to bring him to my new boyfriend's house on Thanksgiving? Geesh.

We made peace and finished cleaning, met the guys in the living room. I had some cookies and brownies baking in the oven to go along with the pies and cakes Scarlett and the others brought. In the meantime, Hunter rolled two joints for everyone to pass around—best Thanksgiving twist of events ever.

I had no problem hanging all over Hunter. Didn't give a fuck about doing it in front of Benji, either. Scarlett's brother teased us about it, but he's the one who caused it. After all, he started it once he sent Hunter a picture of me behind my back.

We all took turns swapping stories while snacking on all the yummy treats we had for dessert. You could tell that Benji was trying to be on his best behavior and thought very carefully before speaking, but overall, he seemed to find his way into conversations well.

Eventually Hunter's roommate called it a night. Scarlett's brother planned on spending the night at Hunter's, so I decided to go so they could have some time to hang out. Then Scarlett and Benji decided to leave. Scarlett asked if I wanted company, but honestly, I really didn't. I told her I was good for tonight, but if everyone wanted to come to my place for Black Friday booze and board games, I would be down to host.

Everyone was down. I told them to come over around one and to bring whatever they wanted. Decided to order pizza and wings for lunch.

Benji and Scarlett headed to their hotel and Hunter walked me out to my car and kissed me goodnight. He had a great time today and so did I. I'm glad he thought to do this; it was a great idea despite the bombshell that was dropped on me.

When I got home, the family was still over, so I had to sneak back into my place; the last thing I wanted was for anyone to see me and want to talk to me after the day I've had.

I took a quick shower and climbed into bed so I could write. I truly did not see this coming… Scarlett and Benji???

Is it weird? Yes, kind of. Is it wrong? Well, no, not really.

Do I think they're perfect for each other? Maybe a better fit than he and I were.

Well, then I guess it's settled. Tomorrow I'll have a better attitude when we're all together.

Entry #105

SCARLETT'S BROTHER AND HUNTER SPENT ALL NIGHT LAST NIGHT GAMING and drinking; I'm glad they had a good time. That's got to be wild, meeting each other in person for the first time after being friends for so many years.

He came over around eleven and laid in bed with me until it was time for everyone to show up. My place is much smaller than Hunter's, but we made it work. Everyone from yesterday was over, plus Hazel and her guy. The food arrived shortly after everyone did, so the timing was perfect. Added a little alcohol to the mix and we were golden.

We played Cards Against Humanity and the conversations turned sexual extremely quickly. We also drank heavily, so let's just say things got a little weird in conversation, but luckily everyone was buzzing enough to not dwell on certain moments the game brought up.

At one point, I got up to refill drinks and Benji followed me into the kitchen. He apologized and said he didn't mean for it to happen, and he promised he didn't have feelings for her while he and I were together. I told him I didn't mind them being together, I just would have appreciated a heads up. I asked him if he was happy, and he said yes. He asked me if I was, and I too said yes. We hugged and that was the end of that. The rest of the afternoon went much more smoothly; I think everyone could feel the space was lighter.

I snuck away to my room to use the bathroom and a little birdie followed me. When I got out, Hunter was sitting on my bed waiting for me. I climbed on his lap and wrapped myself around his body. We were both buzzing and a little handsy, so we fucked real quick before returning to the living room full of guests. We ran the bathroom sink so nobody could hear us.

Hunter's roommate was the first to head out, before Hazel and Max's brother followed. Scarlett's brother didn't want to be a third wheel, so then he tapped out. Benji and Scarlett drank a little too much to safely drive, so he offered to drive them to their hotel and then would meet Hunter back at his place. That worked for me because that meant he and I had a little alone time to finish what we started earlier.

Finally got everyone out of the house, and once they were gone, he and I didn't waste any of the time we had. I am so thankful to be with a man who has a sexual appetite like mine because, damn. What a new world I live in now.

He felt bad about leaving after, but I told him to go have fun with his friend, I really didn't mind. I wanted to write in here for a bit anyway while it's fresh on my mind. Well, it may be tainted with alcohol, but you get the point.

It's eye opening how much can change in a year—to think that last year I was having Thanksgiving dinner with Benji and his family, and now this year I had a Friendsgiving with my new boyfriend in his house, with Benji attending as my best friend's secret plus one that also happened to be her new lover.

Listen, this is going to take me some getting used to, okay?

I mean, he eventually had to move on, and I guess if he was going to move on with anyone, Scarlett wasn't a bad choice. I just hope they don't hurt each other. We've all been friends for so long that if they break up, that could really change the dynamic of our friendship.

Holy shit, I forgot for a little while that we all grew up together. Imagine if Benji and Scarlett had gotten together sooner… how much different would my life have been?

Benji and Scarlett haven't kissed in front of me yet, but they do get close to each other when they're around me. That will be something to process when I actually see it, I think.

Ugh, I need food. TTYL.

Entry #106

SATURDAY NOVEMBER 30TH 2013

I HAD BREAKFAST WITH THE ENTIRE FAMILY AT SOME CAFÉ THIS MORNING before everyone headed home. Nothing glorious happened, but I did want to tell Mom about Scarlett and Benji. Assuming she would tell Dad, I decided to tell them both in the car on the way home (I rode with them because I didn't want to drive).

Mom couldn't believe it and was concerned about how I was feeling. I told her I didn't really care, it just bothered me how I found out but I'm working on moving past it.

Hunter just called and asked if I was up for getting everyone together again at his place later tonight for a bonfire; he ordered a fire pit from a Black Friday deal and picked it up from the store this morning. Of course, I said yes. In the meantime, he's hanging out with Scarlett's brother and I'm enjoying not having to host anyone or wear any clothes. Rocking my bralette, underwear, a long-sleeved cardigan, and thigh-high socks.

FUCK. Scarlett's calling me, I wonder what she wants...

Debating on if I want to answer it or let it go to voicemail in hopes she'll text me what she wants...

I answered. She was calling to ask if I wanted to have lunch with her and Benji "for old times' sake." She even said she'd pick me up so I didn't have to drive, or if I wanted to drive I could, and they'd meet me wherever I wanted to go.

I could tell she was very nervous about inviting me out with them.

Now I feel kind of bad, we're supposed to be best friends. We're all supposed to be best friends…

I agreed to lunch; I thought it would look bad if I didn't. I decided to meet them at Hunter's uncle's place, and since it's near the grocery store, I could knock out some food shopping too.

What should I wear? It's got to be good, but not too good. I don't want them to get the wrong idea.

BRB.

• • •

So first of all, I ran into Max while I was grocery shopping. His hair was not as short as it normally was and he's growing a beard… he looked delicious if I'm being honest. Very mature looking, I almost didn't recognize him.

We exchanged holiday stories and mine totally won as far as drama went. He mentioned how much his parents loved Hazel; I can't wait to tell her that, she'll be so happy.

He asked me if I was still enjoying being in a relationship, and he laughed when I said yes. He responded with, and I quote, "That's a shame, I kind of miss being inside of you." And then he breaks eye contact and moves his shopping cart towards the registers like he didn't just say what he said.

I swear, if I was drinking something I would have spit it out everywhere.

I didn't have to look in a mirror to know that I was beet red in the face. We got in line to check out and I honestly didn't know how to respond to that, so I just didn't say anything.

He then broke the silence with, "I missed you on my birthday."

Turns out his birthday was on the eighteenth; like how could I possibly have known that? I guess that's why Hazel left so early that Saturday… he threw himself a birthday party on the sixteenth because his actual birthday was on a Monday and who wants to party on a Monday?

Not like I would have done anything differently had I known it was his birthday, but yeah, I probably would have shot him a happy birthday text. Though actually, no, I would not have actually—too risky.

So like, I kind of think he's flirting with me? I mean I don't know why; we didn't really know each other long before Hunter and I got together, and it's not like we had intense conversations or anything like that.

Where has this male attention been all my fucking life?

We eventually checked out and he walked with me to my car. He helped me put the groceries in my trunk and said he hopes to see me again, after I thanked him for his help.

So weird.

Anyway, lunch with Scarlett and Benji was… really not that bad. They seem to care for each other and expressed multiple times that they were sorry and had absolutely no feelings for each other prior to the present moment it happened.

I believe them. I mean, I have to believe them. Don't I? I love them, they're my best friends, and I want them to be happy. Now granted, I never imagined them together, I guess it's not the worst thing in the world. Though it is a little weird because I wonder if Benji is comparing me and Scarlett... I need to get out of my head.

It's almost time to get to Hunter's and I still need to figure out something cute to wear. It's in the high sixties right now so it's not that cold out, plus the fire will keep me warm.

· · ·

So it's around two thirty in the morning and I'm still a little drunk. Hunter fought hard to have me spend the night, but I'd rather him hang out with Scarlett's brother while he's in town. After all, they're leaving tomorrow, well, today. And honestly my head is spinning again about this whole Scarlett and Benji thing so it's best I work this out by myself.

I saw them kiss.

I don't think they meant for me to see, but I did. And they both saw that I saw. It was awkward and I kept my distance for the rest of the night.

I saw my best friend kissing my ex-boyfriend. Not jealous, not angry, not upset, just feeling really fucking weirded out by it. It made me question my past relationship with Benji and future relationship with Scarlett.

Maybe she and I need boundaries? About what we will and will not talk about. But she's my best friend, we usually tell each other everything. Or so I thought we did.

Am I now the odd one out? Are they going to move on, get married, and forget about me?

I still love Benji. Not in the same way, but like, he was my first… everything, and we grew up together. We all grew up together. Those kinds of feelings don't just go away.

I have a true connection with Hunter. So then why is this bothering me so much? Maybe I'm just in shock?

What's wrong with me?

I really don't know.

Entry #107

NO SUNDAY BREAKFAST WITH THE PARENTS TODAY, INSTEAD WE ALL GOT together at Hunter's one last time before everyone left. He made us omelets, pancakes, hashbrowns, and I brought some coffee. It was a little awkward at first, but Scarlett's brother helped break the tension by being his charming, obnoxious self. He's kind of a goofball and I can't believe a part of me has missed him.

When it was time for goodbyes, Scarlett pulled me to the side; told me she loves me and hopes this doesn't change things between us. I told her I loved her back, smiled, and hugged her. Benji just looked up at me from a distance, smiled, and walked away like all of our history had suddenly been erased. After everyone had left, Hunter and I went and laid in bed together to chill out for a bit and relax from hosting and socializing.

He asked me if I was feeling any better about the whole Scarlett and Benji thing. I didn't want to lie to him, so I didn't, I just told him it was a little weird and I needed to accept that things are different between us now.

Eventually we changed the subject and got a little more comfortable. He got hard from me wiggling against him to get comfortable, so I gave him head before climbing on top of him and taking control. I pressed down on his chest while he had his hand wrapped around my throat— we had this hold on each other until we finished, it was fucking great.

While I was grabbing us some drinks after, I had an "ah-ha" moment and realized I needed a Christmas tree and some decorations, so we decided to make a day out of it. We stopped by the store for some ornaments and whatever little things I could find for around the house before heading into town for the perfect tree. We went back to my place and Hunter carried in the tree while I brought in all the bags of decorations. We put on some Christmas music to play in the background and decorated the tree together with mugs full of spiced eggnog.

It was literally like a dream. Hunter is the man I want to spend the rest of my life decorating Christmas trees with. I've never been more certain of it than I am now after today. I don't know what was so significant about today, I just know in my heart he is who I want to experience my life with. I wonder if he was thinking the same thing about me.

Tomorrow is back to reality until Christmastime. The same time of year when no one gives a fuck about anything until at least mid-January.

Man, I love this time of year.

Entry #108

SATURDAY DECEMBER 7TH 2013

OH, 'TIS THE SEASON OF MAGIC AND LOVE.

Hunter and I went ice skating at this indoor ice rink with Hazel, Max's brother, and the rest of the girlfriends' group and their guys.

Also, I recently chatted with some of the wives this week. They're all busy with their families doing holiday prep and all the things, so we're going to try and get together again sometime after the new year.

Ice skating was a lot of fun and I'm so glad the day turned out as well as it did. We all met up around twelve and skated for about an hour or so. Only Hazel and Max's brother joined us for lunch; the others went on their separate ways.

During lunch, Hunter got a call and had to run outside and meet someone. I sometimes forget he sells weed and the holidays seem to be pretty busy. Call me crazy because this very well could be a coincidence living in the South, but the truck he ran out to sit in looked oddly similar to Max's. I only had a view of the passenger side so I couldn't see the driver or the license plate. If it was Max, wouldn't his brother have said something?

Even if they do know each other, Hunter and I were just friends fooling around with each other, there was no commitment until the night of my birthday, and since then, I've only been with him. If men are allowed to "sleep around and have fun," then I, as a woman, can do the same. I'm not going to spend another moment stressing about this. I've got to get out of my head.

Max's brother had some work around the farm to do, so he and Hazel parted ways after lunch. Hunter asked about Christmas plans on the way back to my house. To be honest, and like I told him, I haven't even thought about it yet. I'll have to see what the parents have in mind tomorrow morning at breakfast. So, then he asks if he could join us for Sunday breakfast... Benji never asked to join us for Sunday breakfast...

He caught on to my hesitation and asked me about it. It's not that I don't want him there, it's just, I've never had a guy join me and my family for Sunday breakfast before. It just seemed... serious? I texted Mom and she said it was okay, so he's going to spend the night and walk over with me in the morning. He's at his place right now showering and packing a bag. Not going to lie, I'm a little nervous for some one-on-one with the parents. I'll report back tomorrow how things went.

Entry #109

HUNTER JUST LEFT; I KNOW HE KNOWS I WAS ANXIOUS TO WRITE ABOUT today.

So, breakfast went really, really well.

Now that the parents have had some one-on-one time with Hunter, they seem to really like him, and Mom texted me after, letting me know how happy she was for me and that he and I look great together. I guess I could not have asked for a more perfect morning. I was so worried for no reason. Hunter seems to fit in well with the family. Dad even seems to like him too… hell, they made plans to go golfing next summer. I didn't even know Hunter could golf, let alone Dad.

As for the holiday plans, he and I have some thinking to do. The parents are going back home to do Christmas Eve with Mom's side of the family and Christmas Day with Dad's; they're staying through New Year's Day. They told me they would love it if I could make it, Hunter too… even offered to pay for our flight tickets so all we had to worry about was a hotel. Hunter tried to back down on them paying, but the parents insisted, so we told them we'd chat about it and see.

Well, we went back to my place and hung out on the couch, passing a joint back and forth, discussing what we wanted. He liked the idea and it's actually perfect timing given he's out of school for the holiday break from the twentieth to January sixth. As for my schedule, Mom's closing the office from the twenty-fourth to the sixth, so I have some free time also.

We decided to fly up on the evening of the twenty-third and return home on the twenty-seventh. Doesn't leave us much time to find a hotel, so we have to move fast, but I know we'll figure it out.

Hunter has never been to New York City, so we decided to get a hotel right in the middle so we could spend some time sightseeing in between visiting with family. It's going to be great! Oh, and he already has plans for us for New Year's Eve. He said a friend of his throws a NYE bash every year and he's looking forward to sharing the evening with me. Apparently, they are doing fireworks. I definitely want in on that.

I have a lot I need to plan for this trip. I'm really excited for us to go on our first trip together. Now to find a hotel and figure out what I'm going to buy him for Christmas…

Entry #110

I HAVE SOME GOOD NEWS FOR A MONDAY. I FOUND US A HOTEL ROOM right in the middle of the city! It's going to be perfect. A little pricy, but 100% worth it. The parents snagged the flight tickets—we're leaving around dinnertime on the twenty-third so Hunter and I will grab something when we land.

I texted Scarlett and she wants to get together on Christmas Eve, so we made plans to hang out together. I saw Mom's side of the family on Thanksgiving, so I think it'll be okay if I skip out on Christmas Eve this year. Scarlett and Benji are going to meet us in the city so we can check out the area and explore some of the holiday scenery.

Hunter asked if I would be okay with it and yeah, I'm fine with it. It's the only way I can see Scarlett now, so I need to be okay with it. We both moved on and I'm happier than I've ever been, so that's good enough for me. I guess he understands the friendship dynamic, so he was cool with it, though I'm sure it may be a little weird for him, so I made sure he knew how much I appreciated his high spirits.

I decided I'm going to get Hunter a new chef knife set for Christmas by the way, I just need to make sure I pick out the best one.

I can't believe we're going to be spending an entire week together in a different state and we're going to wake up next to each other on Christmas Eve AND Christmas Day. Benji and I spent the holidays together, sure, but it was kind of separated. Like for Christmas we would hang out on Christmas Eve and spend Christmas Day with our families.

DUDE STOP. It really doesn't matter anymore. You've got to stop using Benji as a comparison, it's time to move on.

Entry # |||

THURSDAY DECEMBER 12TH 2013

EH, WORK'S WORK, NOTHING REALLY GOING ON THERE. AUSTIN'S LO LI-cense has now been approved so he was able to print out a copy to hang by his desk. He's so excited and I'm proud of him. He put a lot of work into himself over the summer and these past few months, so I know he's anxious for a bit of rest.

As for me, I did something bold. I messaged Benji and we made plans to have a surprise birthday dinner for Scarlett while I'm in town since her birthday is a week after I leave. As much as I wish I could stay, I'm more excited for what Hunter has in store for us. We're going to do something on the twenty-sixth, so there's time to plan. He asked if I wanted any of the other folks to tag along and I said sure, if he wanted to. It'll be weird to see the people who dropped me after years of friendship, but I'm also totally down to rub my new success in their faces.

Hunter came over after work because he had some stress he needed to release, and since he likes to use sex to relieve his stress, I am totally happy to be on the receiving end of that. I was wearing a rose-colored bralette with matching underwear, a white long-sleeved cardigan with the sleeves rolled up, and white thigh-high socks that had black rings around the top. I left the door unlocked so when he walked in, I was standing in the kitchen sipping on some water. He kicked his shoes off and removed his jacket before heading straight towards me.

He pushed me up against the counter and brushed my hair to one side, exposing my neck. He looked me straight in my eyes, nose pressed up against mine, and told me that I'm beautiful. He also wanted me to know that he loves me and is looking forward to spending Christmas in New York with me.

The sudden romantic gesture had me grinning ear to ear and totally beet red in the face. I couldn't form complete sentences, so I just leaned in to kiss him before he plowed into my pussy with those juicy lips of his.

Once we got the romance out of the way, he took me to my bedroom and we relieved some of that stress he was carrying. Let's just say, by the end of it my jaw was aching, and my pussy was throbbing. We do such great things in bed together.

Neither one of us wanted to part ways after, but it was nearly ten thirty and both of us had things to do in the morning. Sometimes I fantasize about us living together, but then I'm also reminded of the times I enjoy spending alone. I mean he likes to do his own things too, so I guess we would do our own things together? I can binge watch raunchy TV shows in one room while he games in the other.

I don't know why I'm even thinking about this right now. I've only been out on my own for six months, do I really want to give up that experience so soon? I mean I love him, and I can definitely see a future with him, but that doesn't mean I'm ready to give up my space just yet.

I'm overthinking something that isn't even a thought to be thinking right now. What Hunter and I have is working, and that's all that matters. We spend nights together when we can and we're literally about to take a mini trip together. So, it's all good, I just need to re-shift my focus back to living in the present.

Entry #112

FRIDAY DECEMBER 20TH 2013

MAN, I REALLY HATE WHEN I'M ON MY PERIOD. I DON'T ENJOY THE WAY IT makes me feel sometimes. Granted I'm on birth control and it helps most of the time; some cycles, I just want to smash everything around me with a bat. I've just been easily irritated more this week and I don't like feeling that way.

I started posting more frequent blog posts to the work website and that's been an exciting experience. It's nice to be able to share my love of writing with more than just, well, myself. Mom's happy and people around the office have had nice comments to say, so I'll take it.

Oh! Chloe finally reached out to me to see if I wanted to grab lunch with her sometime, we're going to meet up tomorrow. Hunter has to work, so I decided to take her to his uncle's place after yoga. We're going to sweat our asses off doing a hot yoga class and then eat a bunch of fried food after, and I'm really looking forward to it.

The plans for next week regarding Scarlett's surprise birthday dinner have been finalized, same as Christmas and Christmas Eve. The only thing left to figure out is where the hell am I going to take Hunter? I wouldn't call myself a pro when it comes to the city; I've only been there a handful of times and it was really just me passing through. We shall see how this goes.

I know I've told myself before that if I'm not writing consistently then it's because something is wrong, but I don't think that's the way I want to be thinking anymore. I want to focus on quality over quantity.

Entries may be a little longer and hurt my hands sometimes, but I think I like that better than writing about the less exciting days. I don't know, something I am going to start testing out in the new year. I love writing, I really do. I just think I need to focus on writing about different moments.

Oh hey, I weighed myself this morning.

My scale was literally covered in dust, I almost forgot I had it. The last time I had my weight checked was back in July when I met the new primary doctor. Not saying that I started exercising more consistently for weight loss, but it is nice seeing that number on the scale trickle down over time. My energy is up, my clothes fit great, and I feel strong and healthy... I feel more powerful in my skin, and I can honestly say that I do love my body. It may have been through a good bit of trauma, but now that I'm able to genuinely enjoy my life, I can honestly look in the mirror and be happy with the woman looking back at me.

BTW Hunter's spending the night and we're going to binge watch Christmas movies together.

Entry #113

FIRST THINGS FIRST, HOT YOGA IS INTENSE. IT MAKES ME FEEL FANTASTIC, but the amount of sweat that it produces is just so gross. Ten out of ten will do it again, though.

Lunch with Chloe was a little awkward *considering I'm lying to her*, but overall, it went well. Granted anytime you hang out with someone for the first time it can be weird figuring each other out, but for the most part we clicked pretty well. So much, I kind of wish she wasn't Austin's girlfriend because it's not my finest hour having to keep the secret that he and I have kissed once or twice before.

Do the wives know about her yet?

Turns out we both love food, so we ordered a bunch of things and shared. We essentially created our own appetizer buffet at the table. It was so intriguing that Hunter had to get his eyes on it, so he sat down with us for a few minutes and munched off my plate. We had a side of onion rings, fried chicken tenders, a side of french fries, mozzarella sticks, fried pickles, and fried jalapeño poppers. It was absolutely way too much fried food, but it was awesome to pick at.

Of course, when I introduced her, I had to explain who Austin was. And then after that I had this pain in the pit of my stomach because I was reminded that Hunter doesn't know about him.

Ughhhh.

So, yeah. Lunch was cool.

Hunter's coming over tonight.

Is this bothering me so much because I feel like I need to be honest with him to be able to move forward? Or is it just anxiety because there's no reason to bring light to something that never meant anything to begin with?

Fuck me. How do guys do this shit?

Entry #114

MONDAY DECEMBER 23ʳᵈ 2013

I DIDN'T TELL HUNTER ABOUT AUSTIN. I DO NOT NEED TO APOLOGIZE FOR something I did while I was single. And that's the end of that.

Work was so quiet, we left at noon. Probably would have been easier to just have taken the day off, but whatever. I'm crabby. I'm nervous for this getaway.

Benji and I never did anything like this. There's just something so mature about the whole "sexy holiday getaway with your boyfriend." Not that I'm not excited, I'm very excited, I'm just nervous, I don't want to mess anything up. We've practically done this before back home so it's really nothing new to us, I guess it just feels different being away from home. Like nobody knows us up there. We can literally be whoever we want to be. Together.

Did I just call the South my home?

Hunter's here. Time to head to the airport.

• • •

Okay my mood is now way totally better than it was earlier today. Allow me to explain.

Usually, Hunter or I am the one driving, so it's different when you're in the back seat and have free range. No, we did not fool around in the back seat of Mom's car. It was just nice to be able to lean on each other and hold hands without worrying about the steering wheel or anything.

Airport navigating was a nightmare and he saw me get a little hot-headed for the first time. It was about a two-hour flight, so we landed and made it up to our rooms by about ten or so. The parents made it to their hotel a little closer to eleven.

There was a small debate about dinner, but in the end I won. I told him I wasn't going to last in New York a minute longer without eating some real pizza. So, we dropped off our luggage and found a pizza place up the street from the hotel. We got one medium half cheese half pepperoni, one medium supreme, some garlic knots, and mozzarella sticks. I was in food heaven, and he loved it just as much as I knew he would.

So, we got to the room and BTW they had a last-minute cancellation, so they bumped our room up to a room with a larger view. We were moved to the seventeenth floor out of twenty-one, so we got to see a lot more than what we would have on the third floor.

We got back to our room stuffed, tired, and in need of a shower. We showered together in the biggest shower I have ever seen. Hunter wanted to have shower sex, but I had a better idea. It was ballsy, but totally worth it.

I wish my hair wasn't wet, but we opened the blinds, turned off all the lights, and we fucked against the glass windows.

We had sex with a view of New York City behind us. What a rush.

It was a little nerve-wracking at first but once we got it, we were good. It left a lot of prints on the window that had to be cleaned up later, but it was so totally worth it.

I should really get to bed. It's been a long day and tomorrow's Christmas Eve, so I don't want to be tired all day. Plus, Hunter looks really good lying next to me right now. He said he has this weird thing where he likes to sleep naked when he travels, something about the freshly made soft and clean bed sheets on his bare ass.

What a man.

Entry #115

YO, WHAT A NIGHT LAST NIGHT. WE TOTALLY WENT AT IT AGAIN AFTER I PUT this away and turned off the lights for the night.

Checking vacation sex off the nonexistent bucket list.

Obviously, for breakfast I took Hunter to get his first ever New York bagel… I got my usual and he got bacon, egg, and cheese on an everything bagel. The guy at the register wrote "him and hers" on the wrappers so we could tell them apart. It was so cute.

We stopped at another place for coffee before heading back to the hotel room to eat. As suspected, Hunter loved the bagel and now understands my passion for food cooked in New York.

We took our time getting ourselves together while we waited for Scarlett and Benji to arrive. It was a little weird seeing them at first, but that didn't last long. Surprisingly the guys were hitting it off and Scarlett and I were chatting like we haven't skipped a beat.

We walked through Central Park, which was not only Hunter's first time being there but also mine, so sharing that experience together was nice.

Unfortunately, there isn't any snow on the ground right now, but I'm hoping it will change before we leave; maybe a little Christmas magic will do us some good this year. I mean it's fucking freezing out, so why not.

We passed a frozen pond, walked over a bridge, and saw a bunch of Christmas decorations that probably look magical lit up at night. It was fun. We drank warm hot chocolate and ate hot pretzels along the way to help keep us warm. Benji made reservations at this Italian steakhouse for dinner, so we decided to head back to the hotel room to warm up and get ready.

Mom called me to do a quick video chat with her and the family, so I had everyone jump on and I think the cousins were surprised to see Benji until they saw Scarlett was with him.

Wonder what kind of shit I'll hear about that from them.

Not long after that was it time for dinner, so we took a cab over and had a really great time. Hunter picked out my dish for me because I couldn't make up my mind. He chose a steak chimichurri dish for us, and the steak nearly melted in my mouth. Scarlett had lobster ravioli and Benji had veal.

It was a nice evening filled with laughter and good intentions. We crushed three bottles of wine between the four of us; thank goodness none of us had to drive. Granted they had to take a train back home, they were fine, no one was hammered or anything.

Hunter pulled this slick move and paid for everyone's dinner. It was very sweet of him to do, and I'll thank him properly with some vacation head once I'm finished with this.

Entry #116

WAKING UP WITH THE MAN I LOVE NEXT TO ME ON CHRISTMAS MORNING IS a feeling I have definitely been missing out on. Being able to share the coziness of Christmas with someone is so special, I'm really lucky to have him.

Hunter loved his new knife set and laughed because now he knows why my suitcase was so heavy. He thought I was just one of those people who packed their entire closet. I mean he's not wrong, I like having options.

Now guess what he got me?

A heart-shaped necklace with our birth stones intertwined in the center. It's beautiful. Peridot for me and aquamarine for him; he's a March baby. March sixth to be exact.

We had to settle for the hotel lobby breakfast because everything else was closed, before heading out to meet up with the family at the grandparents' house. Of course, they all took notice and loved my new necklace. What was even more fun was the morning he and I spent together having our own little Christmas.

I also finally met his sister and her husband—she video chatted with him before we ate dinner. It was nice to meet someone else in his family.

I've seen his uncle around a time or two at the bar and we've been introduced, but we haven't really talked. He's always super busy.

Anyway. We had a lot of carbs for dinner. Stuffed shells, lasagna, meatballs, garlic bread, and chicken parmesan. Talk about a major food coma. We left about an hour after dinner to head back to the city. It was freezing outside, like freezingg outside, so we were all bundled up with our gloves, hats, and thick ass coats. I even wore a scarf, I was so cold.

I've only been gone for six months; what happened to my tolerance for cold weather, is it gone already??

As cold as we were, I convinced Hunter to let me take him to one more spot before the night ended. I took him to the Rockefeller Center Christmas Tree. The ice-skating rink was closed and there was not a single person in sight, but that Christmas tree lit up Hunter's eyes unlike anything I have ever seen. As much fun as it would have been to experience during the day, nothing could beat the moment we were able to share privately together.

We totally took a picture kissing in front of the tree; it's my new screensaver on my phone and I really love it. I don't know if we're still in the "honeymoon phase" of a new relationship, but like, damn, what we have going on is awesome.

Speaking of awesome, we're back in our room about to get all cozy in bed and see where the night takes us. Which is obviously going to be a combination of Christmas and vacation sex.

Entry # 117

DUDE. GOING BACK TO NORMAL IS GOING TO SUUUUCK. TONIGHT WILL BE the ninth night in a row Hunter and I have spent together…

Should I give him some drawer space? Is it too early for that?

This has got to be a new record. I can't believe he isn't sick of me yet.

Scarlett's birthday dinner was at this fancy Asian fusion place and she was certainly surprised. It was weird seeing the rest of the group, considering they dropped me after I moved away. So let's just say I got my "revenge" when I told them all about my new place, how I spent my summer exploring, and more importantly who the sexy man was that I brought with me.

Which by the way, everyone loved him and his accent. He was the center of attention until I had to remind people why we were all together in the first place.

So, not to sound all so dramatic, but it happened again. Only this time, it was intentional. I saw Scarlett and Benji kiss. This was certainly no chicken-peck we're-in-public kind of kiss, this was a genuine "I truly love you, happy birthday" kind of kiss. The kind of kiss he once used to share with me.

. . .

On another note.

I would like to try something new. Every year on New Year's Eve, I will break down the past year, month by month. I don't know, could be cool to look back on someday. May also be therapeutic. Only one way to find out.

• • •

<u>January:</u>

Poor Scarlett, I practically ruined her birthday. At midnight on New Year's Eve, Benji proposed to me. I couldn't give him a response, so I walked away and left him in the middle of the room until he followed me out into the hallway.

I won't lie, I panicked.

We went back to his place for some privacy so we could talk. I wouldn't say we screamed at each other, but our Northern Italian personalities shined that night.

Once the sun started to rise, we caught on to how much time had passed and realized we were not coming to an agreement anytime soon, and probably never will. At the end of the day, we both knew we wanted different things, and we loved each other enough to set ourselves free.

Don't get me wrong, it was absolutely heartbreaking, but it needed to happen. We couldn't afford to go on any longer for the sake of our hearts. In the end, we had different visions for our happy endings and nothing was going to change that.

I spent all of New Year's Day in bed, crying until I finally managed to fall asleep. I didn't wake up again until the next morning; thankfully I worked the evening shift that night. I couldn't face Benji so soon after the breakup and Scarlett didn't know anything about it at the time, so I ended up missing her birthday. Well, so did Benji, so she thought he and I ignored her and she got upset with me, so I had to tell her the truth.

Her attitude quickly changed, but mine did not. I hung up the phone and spent the rest of the month questioning whether or not breaking up with Benji was the right thing to do.

<u>February:</u>

The parents had a combined birthday bash at the house for their birthdays. Mom's is on the twelfth and Dad's on the seventeenth, so they're pretty close. Ever since they've gotten married, they have a joint party. I kind of think it's sweet.

See, when Benji and I were little, it was obvious to those around us that we had a crush on each other. All throughout elementary school, Benji and I were always in the same class. In junior high and high school, we had less classes together, but we always found a way to see each other anyway.

Neither of us knows why it took us so long to start dating. All we could say was that things happen when they happen for a reason. I guess the timing was finally right or something, who really knows. Maybe curiosity had finally gotten the best of us.

As we got older, our crushes certainly blossomed, as did our curiosities. After all, Benji was my very first kiss back in high school. It was junior prom and he and I were there with our friends. A certain song he introduced me to, that I'm still obsessed with to this day, started playing on the speakers, so he took my hand, and we did our thing on the dance floor.

My first ever slow dance with a guy.

Towards the middle of the song, we made eye contact, and he told me for the first time since us knowing each other that I looked beautiful. I smiled, looked down, then back up at him and told him he looked pretty handsome himself.

He flashed me a smile and asked me if it would be crazy if he kissed me. I blushed so hard my cheeks were hurting, and I could only manage to work up the nerve to say, "No."

He tucked some hair behind my ear before leaning in and pulling me towards his lips with his thumb resting underneath my chin.

My hormones lit up like fireworks.

It was a little awkward at first and it didn't last very long, but it was one I will never forget.

When the song ended, I went back over to the rest of the girls, and he went over to the guys, and all they wanted to know was how it was and what's going to happen next. (Benji and I flirted with each other a lot. Could be why neither of us really dated anyone in high school.)

Back to the point. This was our first Valentine's Day technically apart; previously we always ended up seeing each other either at school or at someone's house for a hangout or whatever. This was the year that all had to stop, because of what I did.

It was incredibly painful.

March:

Feeling a bit better about myself at this point. Decided to quit the shitty retail job I had that was killing my body so I could take a month or two to figure out who I am and what I want to be doing with my life. I did a lot of self-reflection during this month; I wish I started this journal sooner.

April:

Benji's birthday was on the twentieth and I couldn't bring myself to go. We hadn't spoken since we broke up and we hadn't seen each other either. Scarlett wouldn't get in the middle of it so there was no way to know how he was doing. She did go to his birthday party and told me he looked good and that he didn't have a girl with him or anything like that. But that's it.

Spent some time exploring career options. Toyed with the idea of a career in medical sonography or in the law field as a paralegal.

May:

Just when I was feeling somewhat like myself again, my car died on me. The transmission blew and it wasn't worth repairing. Thankfully the parents let me borrow their car around their schedule, but it was still a nightmare. I tried to find a new one but there wasn't anything out there that I wanted. Looking back, I guess it's a good thing, because three weeks later I got the news about the move down here. Shit, I still can't believe how much has changed since the night I found out.

June:

Big, big month of wins.

Bought a new car that was in much better shape than my last.

Bought myself all-new furniture to fill my new home with.

Bought a new wardrobe and began to dress myself in clothes that fit better.

I started putting myself and my needs first. I learned to do things simply because I want to.

I started sleeping with my new weed dealer, who happened to be Scarlett's brother's friend that lived a few houses down from me.

Was then introduced to one of Mom's coworkers, Austin, who turned out to be someone fun to make out with.

<u>July:</u>

While Scarlett and I had a rocky friendship for a little while after I moved, it did start to get a little better as time went on. Distance can be difficult sometimes. Makes it easier to hide things from people.

Hunter introduced me to some of his friends and I became friends with the girls in the group. We started a group chat and hung out together a few times. This is also kind of when I started to develop stronger feelings for Hunter… I kept going back and forth with myself in my head about it. I managed to push those feelings aside so I could continue to find myself and have some fun. This was also the month he and I broke a rule and spent the night together for the first time.

Had my first appointment with my new primary doctor, and that went well, as did the lab work.

Lastly, I started hanging out with Hazel, one of the girls from the girl-friends' group. We get along really well and were the only two stoners in the group, so it's nice to have each other.

<u>August:</u>

Started feeling homesick this month. Benji called me and did my birthday ritual with me. Looking back, that must have been hard for him considering I didn't reach out to him on his.

I turned twenty-five this month. Holy shit! Milestone birthday. Life is getting real.

I met someone new named Max, a fucking weed-growing cowboy. He and I had some fun together for a little bit, but it didn't last long.

This is also the month Hunter and I started dating. On the night of my birthday to be exact.

<u>September:</u>

Shadowed a job role at Mom's office for two weeks then took on a job working full-time. Excited to start something new; it's been enjoyable so far. Also started going to a yoga studio and absolutely loving it.

Hazel had a pregnancy scare and then I had a pregnancy scare.

That messed with my head a good bit.

<u>October:</u>

Thankfully I was not pregnant, and I did eventually get my period. It just so happened to be that I had a very large cyst on my ovary. The cyst resolved on its own, no surgery was needed. Had an impromptu work trip to Chicago that I went on with Austin.

Hunter and I said "I love you" for the first time. Even went on a cute date to the pumpkin patch and took our first picture together.

November:

Work's been kind of slow, but overall, it's going well. A few challenges here and there but nothing that I can't handle.

I had a nightmare about my car accident that led me to telling Hunter about the whole thing.

I told the parents about Hunter and introduced them and the family on Thanksgiving. And then I went with him to his house for the Friendsgiving he was hosting, with Benji showing up as Scarlett's surprise plus one to break the news to me in person that they're in love.

Some emotional spiraling had occurred this month.

December:

Began writing a blog for the website at work, I'm starting to have a little more confidence in myself, and overall life seems to be working out really well for me.

Spent the last eight nights in a row with Hunter for the holidays and tonight will be the ninth for New Year's Eve (which I need to start getting ready for soon).

We celebrated Christmas together and had the craziest sex ever against the hotel glass windows overlooking NYC.

We've grown so close these past few months and even more these past few nights travelling together.

No doubt I'm in love with him. Totally and completely in love with him. I hope he feels the same otherwise I'm screwed.

Big time.

Shit. I really need to get ready for the party tonight. I'm wearing black high-waisted pants with a gold laced body suit, a wine-red-colored choker, and a cute black blazer.

It's forty-one degrees outside. Gross.

BRB. See ya next year, Lucy. Proud of you.

Entry #118

FUCKING HUNTER AND MAX KNOW EACH OTHER.

Max is Hunter's supplier and they've known each other for about two years.

HOW DID I NOT SEE THAT POTENTIAL CONNECTION BEFORE???

Apparently, they didn't get along at first because an old girlfriend of Hunter's broke up with him to be with Max. Eventually Max broke up with her and then he and Hunter bonded over her craziness before going into business together.

Is it possible they've talked about me before without realizing they were both talking about the same person?

Max was a gentleman about it and let me tell Hunter about us. Hunter had some questions, and I answered every single one of them. He acknowledged that he knew I was single, and we didn't exactly finalize things until my birthday, so he can't be upset for something I did before he and I were legit. He seemed to understand.

My stomach started to hurt when Hazel walked up to us and pulled me away so I could walk and talk with her. I spilled the beans, but honestly, she's the only one who really knew this whole time. I looked back and glanced at Hunter, and he was there with Max and his brother talking.

But like if they've been hanging out for ALMOST TWO YEARS, how could he possibly have not known who Max's brother was??? Was he in college or something??

WHAT THE FUCK MAN, WHAT'S THE MISSING PIECE AND HOW DO I EVEN BRING THAT KIND OF QUESTION UP?

Hazel brought me over to the alcohol; I made a drink for myself and one for Hunter. I brought it over to him and we talked a little more and I apologized again. He told me it was fine; it was just a little awkward for a few minutes but then we bounced back to our old selves, at least I thought we had.

We kissed each other at midnight but there wasn't as much passion as I was hoping for. My heart sank into my chest. I legit wanted to cry. Our first midnight New Year's Eve kiss was ruined. There were no fireworks either because it rained.

On the way back to my place, the drive was kind of quiet. He still stayed the night but there was no holiday sex or any major touching really. We kissed goodnight, said I love you, and went to bed. I could definitely tell that something was wrong.

This morning when I woke up, Hunter was in the shower, so I went in the kitchen to make some coffee and breakfast. I'm flipping pancakes with my right hand and sipping on coffee with my left when he comes up from behind me and hugs me.

He asked me to turn around for a second and so I did. He apologized and felt bad for the way he treated me since he found out about Max.

He said he was reminded of the feelings he had when an ex left him for Max, and he was worried the same thing was going to happen again.

I put my coffee down and grabbed his cheeks, pulling his face in close to mine, front and center. I told him there was absolutely no chance of that ever happening and explained how I wasn't into Max that way from the beginning and that I ended it quickly because of my feelings for him.

He kissed me with some oomph in it this time. And then we spent about an hour having make up sex before moving our party over to the living room so we could relax for the day. We eventually had some lunch delivered. We ordered burgers, fries, onion rings, and BBQ/buffalo chicken tenders. It was so good; we ordered way too much food.

Hazel texted me something that I can't get out of my head. She said, "When you truly love someone and want to be with them, who they were before you got together doesn't matter anymore, and dwelling on the past certainly won't help anything move forward in the present."

Shit. I've got to call Scarlett for her birthday tomorrow.

Oh by the way, the parents are back home.

MONDAY JANUARY 20TH 2014

SOO WHO KNEW WE HAD OFF WORK TODAY FOR MARTIN LUTHER KING JR. Day, because I sure as hell did not.

I woke up this morning and went on about my normal day. Hit up yoga in the morning (didn't see Austin or Chloe) and had legit the best playlist going as I drove home and got myself together for work. Period ended and I was feeling good about myself again, so I put on some jeans (the ones with a flare on the bottom), a cute beige sweater, and those new boots I got (the ones with the four-inch heel).

I decided to take my coffee to go and drank it on my way to the office. Mind you my killer playlist was still going, and the sky was a beautiful shade of blue. The kind that makes you want to feel the warmth of the sun on your face all day. Well, I pulled up to an empty parking lot and literally was like, "What the fuck, where is everyone?"

I called Mom but she didn't answer so I texted Austin, and he didn't respond. I headed home, and by the time I was around the corner from my place, Mom called and told me the office was closed for the holiday. I was like, "Well nobody told me." All she said was, "Oops."

I didn't want to waste a cute outfit, plus my makeup came out really good today so I was hesitant to wash it all off. I went inside, put my stuff down, and texted Hunter to see what he had going on. He called me within five minutes; turns out he knew about the holiday because he's off from class, but he's working tonight.

He already had plans to game and kind of fuck around for the day before work, and I didn't want to get in the way of that, so I decided to stay home and fuck around myself, but in sweatpants instead of jeans. I decided I wasn't going to leave the house for anything.

I took an edible and sprawled out on the couch, watching back-to-back cheesy romcoms until I got hungry. I wasn't feeling anything in my fridge, so I had some chicken lo mein, dumplings, and crab rangoon delivered.

It was amazing.

Halfway into stuffing my face with the best Chinese food I can find; I heard police sirens outside my front door.

I was DEFINITELY paranoid, just thankful I had a candle burning and chose an edible over smoking. I peeked out a window and saw five cop cars sitting in the middle of the street right outside my house! They had two K9 units and I saw an officer walking up to the parents' front door... after they received no response, they started walking over to mine and of course I started freaking out, so I moved away from the window and quickly pulled myself together.

There was a knock on my door. I was super worried about being caught high, so I only cracked open the door while talking to the cop.

Turns out there was an altercation a few houses down from me, so they were reaching out to the neighbors to not only see if we had seen/heard anything, but to tell us to stay inside with all the windows and doors locked until they found the guy responsible for attacking somebody. He wouldn't get into specifics, but he said the guy on the run is considered armed and dangerous.

He handed me a business card and said to call if I saw or heard anything suspicious.

Who knew cops had business cards?

Anyway, I did what he said and texted the parents to let them know what was going on, then called Hunter to warn him so he wasn't caught by surprise if they go down to his place.

He was sweet; he asked me if I felt safe and if I needed him to come over, but I was fine. I went back to my cheesy romcoms and continued stuffing my face with delicious Chinese food.

I went on with my day, but after the second movie I got a little bored laying on the couch, and the edible wore off, so I was feeling kind of bleh. Granted I told myself earlier I wasn't going to leave the house, now I kind of can't because there's a psycho on the loose in my neighborhood.

I started cleaning up from lunch when Dad called to check in on me. Told me he and Mom would be back later this evening and that I could join them for dinner if I wanted. I accepted.

Fast forward, we were all sitting around the kitchen island eating dinner when we heard a very loud bang, like something had blown up. Dad said it sounded like a transformer blew, but when we looked out the window to peek around, the fucking neighbor's car was on fire! That must have been the house that had the altercation...

Mom called 911 and Dad walked with me over to my place so I could get the business card to call the cop that came by earlier. He answered right away and within five minutes there were a bunch of cop cars and a fire truck out front. Now get this, the guy they were looking for was found in the motherfucking treehouse! He hurt himself setting the car on fire so the K9 dogs were able to trace his scent.

Fucking nuts, right? We heard the story on the news about an hour later and that's how we found out how it all ended.

What hurts the most about this entire ordeal? The city condemned the treehouse for evidence and now it's a threat to public health because the guy they caught practically bled all over it. Since it's so old, they're going to knock it down once they're done with it. It's so sad.

Hunter called me when he got off work to check in and I filled him in on the details. He told me that treehouse has been around since he was a teenager, so he's sad to see it go. To help make him feel better, I suggested he should build one in his backyard after graduation. Maybe even add a bar in there or something for entertainment. He loved the idea.

Entry #120

SUPERBOWL SUNDAY!

Couldn't tell you who was playing or which team won, but I can say that Superbowl Sunday is a new favorite holiday to party on. Between the food, drinks, and the vibes, it's a decent time.

I can't believe I've never paid attention before; I feel so sheltered.

So, I was a little surprised, but we watched the game at Max's house. He hosts and Hunter attended last year so he wanted to keep up with the tradition. I didn't want to ruin that or get in the way, so I told him I was totally cool to go if he was.

Hazel was there and luckily for me, she is as clueless about football as I am, so we bonded over that. A few other people showed up, but not many. I didn't know Hunter was as into football as he is; now I feel kind of bad because we haven't watched any games together... looks like I need to learn football. Better yet, I'll just have him teach me.

Max was by himself all night. Hazel mentioned he's been keeping to himself, at least from what she's seen. I guess I shouldn't feel too bad considering he doesn't even want to be in a relationship.

We had pizza, wings, and multiple types of dips to snack on throughout the evening. Hazel and I drank wine and the guys pounded beer. After the halftime show, a few people dipped out, so it was just down to the five of us... me, Hunter, Hazel, Max, and his brother.

Max's brother got to the drunk stage where he couldn't keep his thoughts to himself... so he and Hazel took that all too familiar-looking walk of shame back to his room to "go finish watching the game in there."

So then it was just down to the three of us... me, Hunter, and Max, all alone on the couch together.

For visual purposes, Max was on the left end of the couch, Hunter on the right, and I was on Hunter's left, so I was technically in the middle of the two of them but there was a fair amount of space between Max and I. Hazel was on my left and Max's brother was on her left next to Max.

Before they left the room, we all had passed around a thick ass blunt, so by the time it sunk in that I was alone with Hunter and Max, my high was peaking.

I got sooo quiet; luckily nobody noticed, so I had enough time to sit in my thoughts for a moment and let the words flow in and out...

I've never been in a threesome, but I have fantasized about it a time or two. Though I'm the jealous type so I would have to be single to feel more comfortable about being in a threesome. Maybe. However, if I ever were to participate in one, it for sure as fuck would be with Hunter and Max.

I had to stop the thoughts because I found myself looking back and forth between the two of them as I was in my head, and I didn't want anyone to notice.

Hopefully no one noticed.

When a commercial came on, Hunter excused himself to use the bathroom, so it was just Max and I sitting on the couch together. Considering the comment he made when we ran into each other at the grocery store a few months back, I was... a little on edge. Especially given now that he knows I'm Hunter's.

Wonder why it didn't feel this weird on NYE? Maybe because there were more people there?

I played on my phone to avoid engaging in conversation, but most importantly, I felt the giggles coming on and this was 100% not the best time for that.

Max got up and went to the kitchen for more beer, asked me if I needed anything, and I said no. Then he asked me if I was thinking the same thing he was thinking.

I'M LIKE, WHAT IN THE FUCK DID HE JUST SAY?

I then flashed him a look and I do hope it was a look of confusion and not curiosity... that was totally unexpected, especially given his and Hunter's history.

Hunter came back and sat down next to me. Kissed me and asked how I was doing. I told him how high I was feeling, and he laughed for a second before going to get me some water. He came back and told me to drink something nonalcoholic and to sit back and relax right up against him. I did exactly as I was told, and I was so comfortable next to him, I could have totally fallen asleep.

Too bad my mind was totally obsessed with wondering what the fuck Max meant by what he said... made me wonder if he caught on to the thoughts in my head.

Fuck.

I tried to ignore it and focus on the game in front of me, but I had no clue what was happening anyway, and fantasizing seemed like a way better use of my high than watching football.

So, would it happen on the couch? Would we go to Max's room? Or would we take it to mine or Hunter's place? Maybe to my place so it's a mutual space?

Okay so let's say we're at my place, but like where in my place? My couch might just barely fit the three of us. My bed, I do have a king size so I'm sure that'll work. But like, what if it doesn't go well… I can't just get a new bed, can I?

Sooo like, what if they both just took care of me, and I took care of them? What if Max went down on me while I was giving Hunter head? Or Hunter is inside of me and I'm giving Max head? Just thinking again of all the possible things we could do together is making me fucking WET.

Back to reality—towards the end of the game, Hazel and Max's brother resurfaced so we all waited around for the game to end so we could help clean up and head out. I cleaned with Hazel and got as far away from the guys as I could.

Hunter and I left shortly after, and he dropped me off at my place. As much as I wish we could have spent the night together, I'm glad we didn't so I could get in here and get this all down while it's fresh.

Though after tonight, I should really put this threesome fantasy to rest. I couldn't do it anyway, let's be real here—I don't have it in me. And even if I thought I could, there's no way the two of them would even go for it given what happened between them previously.

Entry #121

AFTER THE NEIGHBOR FIASCO, WORK STARTED TO PICK BACK UP AND I went back to working forty hours a week. While my bank account is thankful, I had to redo my morning and evening routine, which took about a week or so to get used to.

Anyway, Hunter just left. The parents had their joint birthday dinner tonight at this seafood place they like going to. They spent all day together and then the four of us had dinner together, it was nice. Mom liked the new pocketbook I bought her, and Dad liked his whiskey set that Hunter helped pick out for him.

This year, Valentine's Day was on a Friday night, so we spent the entire weekend together at my place. Hunter's roommate has a girlfriend now and she stayed over for the weekend, so he and I spent the weekend at my place so we could all enjoy some privacy.

Friday was a pretty hectic day at work. Everyone everywhere needed something and they all needed it done within that split second of telling me what they needed. It was not an enjoyable workday.

Around three o'clock some guy walked in with this gorgeous bouquet of flowers and a purple envelope attached. Austin was the closest, so he walked up to the guy to see who he was looking for... me being the nosey person I am, I watched the entire interaction from behind my computer screen.

Austin called me over to tell me the delivery was for me, and I tried so damn hard to cover up my cheesy smile, but I failed.

I went back to my desk and of course everyone was watching me. The flowers were simply gorgeous… couldn't tell you what was in it, but I know for sure there were some roses. There were hints of baby blue, lavender, soft pink, purple, and white colored flowers.

In the envelope it read, "Happy Valentine's Day, Lucy. This is only the beginning… just you wait and see what I have in store for you tonight. Love you! Hunter."

Dude, I blushed so damn hard, I could not hold in my feelings whatsoever. Hunter was in class so I couldn't call him; instead I sent him a text thanking him for the flowers and letting him know how excited I was to see him later that night.

It was so hard to get back into work mode after that, but I managed.

He still won't tell me how he did it, I bet he asked the parents to let him in, but when I came home from work later that day, there was a tent set up in my living room made out of blankets and chairs, with pillows underneath and rose petals scattered all throughout the room.

On the kitchen table was a heart-shaped box of chocolates and a bottle of wine with two glasses next to it and another note attached. It said, "Put on something cute, pour yourself a glass of wine, and settle in for the night. I'll be back from the store soon to cook us some dinner. Love you."

I bolted to my room so I could take a quick shower and feel shower fresh, because obviously there was crazy sex to be had after all that. I had to thank him somehow.

Fast forward, when he walks in, I'm standing in the kitchen rolling us a joint while I'm sipping on some wine. Didn't even have time to lay in a sexy position before he walked in, but oh well. I was ballsy, yo. I got this sexy red outfit that pretty much wraps around me like a bow, barely covering anything. It legit took me about five minutes to figure out how to wrap myself in it, only for Hunter to have it off me within seconds.

After some long-awaited Valentine's Day pleasures on both our parts, we changed clothes into something more comfortable and resumed our evening that he had planned for us. He made us steak and lobster and wouldn't let me touch a thing, so I fed him wine, weed, and chocolate in between.

We had dinner and watched a movie underneath the tent he made for us. It was a perfect evening and I almost forgot to give him the gift I got him! I got him a new gaming headset that Scarlett's brother mentioned he has talked about for some time.

We spent the rest of our evening cross buzzing and having the best time together. As the wine and weed did its thing, our curiosity for each other's bodies took over and the next thing we knew, we were underneath the tent naked, covering each other in chocolate syrup so we could lick it off.

It made a huge mess, but nothing a load of laundry couldn't handle...

He licked syrup off my boobs, my stomach, and even went near my inner thighs like he was going to go down on me, but instead kept teasing me with his tongue. I was tired of being teased so I took over and started doing it to him, though I actually did lick chocolate syrup off his dick and that was as much fun for me as it was for him.

We had already made a mess so nothing else really mattered at that point. We moved over to the dining room table for some extra room because missionary was not going to satisfy the hunger for each other we just built up.

I was lying on my back with my legs resting over his shoulders while his hand was wrapped around my throat, his thumb pressed against my lips, waiting for me to suck on it, as he was plowing into me like we had never done it before. After we finished, we took a shower before heading to the bedroom for the night.

This is going to sound incredibly cheesy, but he made me feel so special today; we had a magical time and I'm so grateful for him. I fucking love him, I can't believe he's mine and I'm his. Talk about a hell of a way to celebrate our first Valentine's Day together.

BRB Scarlett's calling me.

Uh… I really don't know how to say this because I'm still processing it, but Benji proposed to Scarlett on Valentine's Day, and she said yes. It's weird because in another universe, that was supposed to be me. It's also weird because they haven't been together for very long. I mean granted we all kind of grew up together, I guess I just didn't see this happening so soon after them getting together.

I am happy for them; it just feels a little weird. They're my best friends from childhood for fuck's sake… Benji even gave her his grandma's ring, the same one he proposed to me with. AKA the same grandma who taught me the birthday ritual I've been doing for years and who wanted me to have her ring from the moment we first met.

I said my congrats and got off the phone as soon as I possibly could. Benji's parents were out of town for the holiday, so he closed the restaurant an hour early and had a candlelit dinner prepared for the two of them. Scarlett said there were flowers and candles scattered all across the restaurant dining area.

They weren't properly dressed for the occasion because they both worked all day. He had her run to the store for something and set it all up while she was gone, so by the time she returned, she walked into an empty restaurant covered in candles and flowers with a table setting for just the two of them.

She sounded really happy and I'm truly excited for them. Just didn't see it coming so soon is all.

I had more that I wanted to write about, but I think I just need to walk away from my thoughts for the night.

Entry #122

FRIDAY FEBRUARY 21ˢᵗ 2014

IT FEELS LIKE IT'S BEEN FOREVER SINCE WE'VE TALKED/HUNG OUT, BUT I met up with the wives tonight for a little Galentine's dinner at one of their houses. We each brought a different-themed charcuterie board and they all turned out amazing. We had so many kinds of desserts and appetizers to choose from, not to mention the signature drink was ON POINT. Almost had to have Hunter come pick me up but I sobered up enough to drive home. The signature drink was this pinkish-looking thing and it tasted so good I could barely taste any alcohol, which is why I drank so much of it. It was a blast—I was happy to have been invited.

I was sitting on the counter sipping on some water when Hunter walked in the door. I wasn't wearing anything sexy or whatever, just a pair of shorts and a bralette with a cardigan. The cozy vibes were strong. I unlocked the door for him when I went to go change and wash my face, so I was like ready for bed by the time he got here. It was a little after eleven, he had to work a little later than expected.

He walked in and took off his shoes and his jacket before walking over to me. I poured him a glass, but before he took a sip of it, he leaned into me and pressed his nose up against mine. I had been drinking, and him being all cute and romantic with me was making me feel bubbly inside. He starts smiling and I start smiling and next thing I know we're hugging each other and having a conversation like we were exactly where we were supposed to be.

"

We moved over to my bedroom and laid together with a movie on. He fell asleep about halfway in, so I figured it was the perfect opportunity to get in here.

Every decision I have made led me to where I am today, and I could not be more grateful to have him in my life. We've known each other for eight months now and things only get better as time goes on. I'm thankful we have the kind of relationship where we can be who we are without having to pretend. Hunter and I have the kind of relationship where we want to see the other succeed, we want to help each other grow and become all that we can be, together.

When Hunter and I made it official, he promised me that us being together would be a power move and not a distraction. Here we are nearly six months later, and he kept his word. I feel stronger and more supported being with him. He's always rooting in my corner, and I in his. Couldn't ask for a better relationship.

Entry #123

SUNDAY FEBRUARY 23RD 2014

BREAKFAST WITH THE PARENTS THIS MORNING WAS NICE. THEY ASKED about Hunter, which was sweet. I did tell him about Scarlett and Benji by the way—he mainly asked how I felt about it but otherwise sent his congrats. When I told the parents, Mom was totally blindsided and did not at all see that coming either.

Hazel and I hung out yesterday and got mani-pedis. Hunter's birthday is practically around the corner, so I'm trying to figure out something fun to do. His birthday is on a Thursday this year, so we'll have to save the fun for the weekend.

Hazel mentioned something about how the guys have gotten together in the past for some paintball; I've never tried it before, so I figured why not, and booked a time slot for that Saturday the eighth.

I went back and forth on whether I wanted it to be a surprise or not, but I decided to tell him so he could invite whoever he wanted. He was stoked. Now to come up with a sexy surprise for later that night…

Earlier while Hazel and I were getting our nails done, she asked me about Superbowl Sunday and what it was like being alone with Hunter and Max in the same room. I was hoping that wasn't ever going to come up again.

We smoked before we went in the salon, so there was no hiding my blushed face and giggles. I flat out told her nothing happened, because nothing did happen, and just said it was weird being in the same room together because it makes me feel bad, but I honestly had no idea they knew each other... had I known, I never would have hung out with Max.

Hazel flat out asked me if I've ever had a threesome before. Apparently, she has before and all she had to say about it was, "Worth it." While I was curious to hear more about her experience, it wasn't the time or place, so we changed the subject.

Are threesomes a Southern thing, or was I just hanging with a different crowd back in NY?

Entry #124

SATURDAY MARCH 1ST 2014

TODAY WAS A BEAUTIFUL DAY. IT WAS SUNNY AND IN THE LOW EIGHTIES with a nice breeze. Perfect opportunity for a mid-morning bike ride.

I cruised around the neighborhood for about an hour; it's weird no longer seeing the treehouse standing. It wasn't in my life for nearly as long as it was for others, but it carried some fun memories that I'm glad I got to experience.

The first bike ride of the season made me feel a little tense, so I rushed over for the final yoga class of the day to get in a good stretch. I ran into Chloe, so she and I grabbed lunch for a little bit after. She gave me the inside scoop I didn't know I needed regarding her relationship with Austin.

I guess he never told her about he and I—which honestly is a good thing because it really didn't mean anything and Chloe's a good friend I'd like to keep around.

Long story short, she dove into their sex life a little bit, and while Austin and I never made it that far, it doesn't mean I didn't think about it during our time together.

Let's just say he made her squirt for the first time in her life by doing things I didn't even know could happen.

While I'm always down for the inside scoop on all things sex related, she probably should have kept half of that story to herself. But damn, am I painfully curious about trying those things out with Hunter now.

We went our separate ways after about an hour of catching up. Hunter and I have been texting back and forth all day, but now I was feeling some type of way, so I started to shift the conversation into a more sexual direction; we teased each other up until after dinnertime when he got off work.

It was painful having to wait so long.

When he called me to say that he was on his way over, I unlocked the front door and headed for the bathtub. We switched over to video chatting after he heard me start the bath, so while he was driving, I undressed for him and got in the tub.

Hunter hung up when he got to the front door. He grabbed a bottle of wine and some glasses from the kitchen on his way over to meet me.

Before he came in, he poured us each a glass. He was sitting behind me in the tub and so I was resting my back up against his chest, sitting in between his legs. Maybe about a minute or so after getting settled, we got a little curious with our free hands, so we chugged our wine and got busy.

He started at the top of my body, moving my hair over to one side, then kissing the opposite, slowly across the back of my neck and out to my shoulder.

The water was warm, but sure enough the man still gave me the fucking goosebumps.

Guess what happens next?

I still can't even fucking believe I agreed to do this.

After he kissed the tip of my shoulder, he paused for a second before asking if I wanted to see this new toy he bought for us to use. Not going to lie, I was a little thrown at first, until my curiosity got the best of me and so I asked questions.

He got this waterproof clit-sucking wand thingy, and it fucking made me scream. I'm great at getting myself off, I take very good care of myself in that department, but damn, this was a whole new experience for me. Hunter too… I know he got a kick out of using that thing on me. We finished our bath and moved to my bed so we could finish things off a little more comfortably. He bent me over the bed and fucked me from behind with my hair balled up in his fist. It was fantastic.

We cleaned up and met back in bed; he had a joint burning when I returned from the bathroom.

As soon as the weed settled in and we started to relax some, I couldn't help myself but ask him back-to-back questions about the toy he bought. I wanted to know the origination story. He laughed and bragged for a second about how good of an idea it was, and obviously I agreed. He mentioned he drove past a sex shop and got curious, so he looked online and found it, and ordered it for us to try. He said he didn't want to go into the store by himself but would totally go with me whenever I wanted.

Keeping that in my back pocket for a rainy day.

The conversation shifted when the munchies kicked in. It wasn't terribly late, so we ordered some pizza. I sure as hell worked up an appetite after going through what he put me through.

Fuck I can't wait to use that thing again... Maybe I'll get lucky one more time tonight.

Entry #125

TODAY IS GOOD OLE ASH WEDNESDAY. I HAVEN'T ATTENDED CHURCH SINCE I was little, so I don't get the ashes on my forehead, but I do participate in Lent. Which means no meat today and every Friday until Easter, which isn't until April twentieth... AKA Benji's birthday AND four twenty. Sounds like forever from now, but it'll be okay. I just have to figure out what I'm giving up this year.

Actually, I think I want to make reading more of a priority instead of giving something up... yeah, that's what I'm going to do. For the next forty days, I am going to read for at least thirty minutes each day. I've got a pile of books I need to get through, so let's fucking gooooo.

Entry #126

LOTS TO CATCH UP ON, SO LET'S GET TO IT.

Hunter turned twenty-nine on Thursday. Guess who also had a birthday? Austin. When I walked into work on Friday, there were birthday balloons and a cake in the fridge for him.

I felt kind of bad that I didn't know, especially considering what he did for me on mine, but I had no idea. I decided to get him a gift card so he and Chloe could have a nice night out.

Hunter couldn't skip class on Thursday because they had an important exam prep in one of his classes, so we met up after I got off work and I took him to a Brazilian steakhouse for dinner. Turns out he had been dying to go to this place for some time, so I definitely scored some girl-friend brownie points with him.

We both had to be up early the next day, so we went back to my place and kept the drinks down to a minimum. Granted we crushed two bottles of wine together, at least it wasn't liquor.

For his sexy birthday surprise, I finally did what I've been dying to try for some time—just been nervous to do it, so I've been procrastinating a little to save it for the right occasion.

I covered my boobs in whipped cream then dipped them in rainbow sprinkles for a sweet birthday surprise. I was otherwise naked, so I walked right out in front of him and within a matter of seconds his face was covered in whipped cream and sprinkles. We made a huge mess, but it was so totally worth it.

Now for his birthday party.

We had a freakin' blast playing paintball and I definitely learned a thing or two about Southern boys and paintball guns… felt like I was in the middle of one of their video games, for fuck's sake. I did get hit in the head and that wasn't pleasant, but all in all it was a great afternoon and Hunter enjoyed himself, so that's what matters. There were about eight of us there, so it was a decent-sized group. I mainly kept up with Hazel the entire time. Thankfully Max didn't show up; I haven't seen him since Superbowl Sunday.

We parted ways after so we could all get cleaned up before we had dinner at this seafood place Hunter loves. Naturally we went back to my place to get ready so we could shower together and whatnot. I love catching him looking at me while I'm getting ready and him catching me doing the same to him. He's so damn sexy, it's hard to keep my eyes off of him sometimes.

Hunter spent the night at my place and thankfully was off Sunday morning, so he and I slept in and ended up having a late breakfast with the parents. We made some coffee then headed over there with our coffee mugs; it was kind of nice all being together. It's like the best of both worlds now that Hunter and the parents have met.

He left for work not too long ago, a little after we had lunch so he could go home and change before he had to be in. I didn't plan anything for dinner, so I checked in with Mom. They were planning on going out for Chinese, so I tagged along with them. She gushed about how much she likes Hunter and Dad mentioned wanting to get to know him better too.

Living separately definitely has changed things between us. Not that we've had issues before, it's just nice having the space I have now and not feeling like I need to constantly explain everything to them.

Anywho. I'm looking forward to work tomorrow. Mom mentioned at dinner she has some good news to share and I'm excited to hear what it is. I have a feeling she's promoting me to full-time processing. While I'm a bit nervous to take on the responsibility, I know I can do it. Plus, I'm going to learn SO much more with the hands-on experience I'll have. I'm looking forward to the challenge.

I don't think I've mentioned it in a while, but I sure am grateful for all the opportunities I've received these past few months.

Shit, come to think about it, it's been nine months since we left New York. Nine whole months since I've moved away from the only life I've ever known. And to think I almost stayed behind... who even knows where I would be right now had I not moved. To be honest, I really don't even want to think about it. I don't care anymore to even fantasize about it either. I could never go back to the life I was living before, and I pray I never have to.

Entry #127

GUESS WHO GOT PROMOTED!

Starting tomorrow, I am being moved into processing full-time!! I'm so excited.

I've only been in the industry for six months and I'm already being promoted. I also got a pretty sweet pay raise; I'm now making twenty an hour! Holy shit yo, I'm stoked.

My responsibilities are just about tripling, but I know I can handle it. Instead of just ordering third party conditions, now I will be disclosing the loan and working with the borrower directly to help get their loan conditions fulfilled. I'll even be working directly with underwriters now.

It's a lot of work I hear, but I can do it. I like staying busy. I'm also excited to learn more aspects of the industry so I can start to get a better idea of where I want to end up. But that's a long ways away, so for now, I'll just focus on learning each new step at a time.

Damn, I can't believe I fucking made it without having to go to college. So many people told me I was going to fail for not getting a degree… well, look who's succeeding now with flying colors, motherfuckers.

Entry #128

ST. PATRICK'S DAY!

Man, work was fun today. We had signature tacos brought in for lunch and everyone wore green. Mom even did a raffle for everyone that was dressed up, and the winner received two extra days of PTO. Unfortunately, I didn't win; one of the processors for another loan officer won. Honestly, she really deserves it though, she works way too hard.

I don't talk to her much, but I probably should now that I'm processing full-time. So far, it's been kind of boring learning the new role and responsibilities, but overall, it's going well. Austin's a great teacher so I'm thankful for that. It was a little weird being alone with him in his office for a couple of hours though, now knowing what I know about him in bed.

Oh, so over the weekend, the guy with the beach house had this huge St. Patrick's Day party Saturday night.

Hazel and I matched outfits. We wore these dark-green, sparkly fringe dresses that came up to our mid-thighs. We looked sexy and our guys were DEFINTELY enjoying our outfit choices. She and I got ready together at her place and met the guys at the party.

Most people hung out inside for the night until it got dark out and someone started a fire. It was a little loud and a bigger crowd than I expected to be around, but I still managed to have a good time.

Hunter and I got a little drunk and a little too handsy. At one point, we totally went back to his jeep and fooled around—hopefully nobody noticed, but if they did, oh well. I mean how could he keep his hands off me, I looked fucking hot. Which he did too—he was wearing his usual jeans and a bright-green shirt with a green hat. His hat was backwards all night, so of course I've been weak in my knees from the moment we laid eyes on each other. And those fucking jeans man, they make him look so tall and strong. Maybe that's why I'm obsessed with seeing him in jeans.

I've got to admit. I really love dressing up and going to parties. I don't love huge crowds, but it is fun getting together with people from time to time. I enjoy the dressing up part the most, I think. Just feels good to finally enjoy my body.

Couldn't tell you what time we got home from the party, but I do know it was really late. I ended up driving us home because Hunter was feeling the alcohol a little more than I was. We made it home just fine and even had sex again before passing out together, it was great.

Entry #129

SPRING IS FINALLY HERE!

It's about sixty-eight degrees right now. A little cloudy, but for the most part a beautiful day. Hunter had to work this morning, so I had breakfast with the parents and spent some time with them until about noon. Now it's a little after one and I'm outside sitting at my purple table writing, covered up wearing Hunter's hoodie, a bralette, and shorts. Life is pretty good right now.

Scarlett and I have been texting a lot lately. She asked if I wanted to help her plan her engagement party in June and of course I said yes. Yeah, it's a little weird for me, but she's my best friend and she's getting married… I need to fucking let it go already.

Processing loans full-time starts tomorrow. Finally, after nearly three weeks of training I'm on my own. I'm a little nervous but I've been paying a lot of attention and created very detailed notes to help guide me along the way if I get stuck. Plus, I know how and when to ask for help, so I know I will be just fine.

I'm a little jealous because I wish I could spend some time with him, but Hunter's off this week from school for spring break. He's mostly going to spend it working, but he may take a day or two to catch up on gaming for a bit. I think he should, he could use a break. Maybe next year we can plan a mini vacation. Fuck, I can't believe it's the end of March already. Summer will be here before we know it.

Entry #130

WELL.

I received my first three loans this week as a full-time processor… literally came in back-to-back, all closing within the first few days in May. I'm excited to get to work but DAMN now that I'm finally in the role I can feel the intensity. Just so many people are involved in these deals, it's imperative to not screw anything up.

I'm happy to share that I have been doing well with reading every day for thirty minutes—only fifteen more days to go until Lent is over, but I think this is something I'll be keeping in my daily routine moving forward. Currently reading a romance novel between two people in a small town and I'm really loving the author's style of writing; I'll have to get more of her books.

Hunter certainly enjoyed his week off. He mostly gamed and worked here and there, but we did end up spending some evenings together. His roommate mentioned he is moving out to live with his girlfriend close to graduation time, so it'll be cool to spend more time over at his place. Not that I don't mind being at mine, it's just fun to change up scenery sometimes.

Hey, so… What if Hunter asks me to move in with him? I know it's a bit of a stretch considering we've only known each other for ten months… but like, in a way we've practically been living together since we started hanging out, considering how much time we spend together. Living together would certainly make things a little easier, but like, are we there yet?

Am I there yet?

Am I ready to give up my own space? Is he? Especially with no longer having a roommate around?

It's not like I had this strong desire growing up to be out on my own, but as I get older, I certainly appreciate some solid privacy, and now that I have it, it's been one of my greatest blessings. Now yes, granted I am still attached to the parents' house, I still have my own separate space and we've made it work for the last ten months without any issues, so I expect the same to continue. Plus, I spent a decent penny when I bought all the furniture to furnish the place... is that something I really want to throw away? No, not really...

Eh.

I do love Hunter and I can see myself living with him, I'm just not sure if I'm ready to move in with him yet. I've never lived with a guy before and I'm not sure how to coexist with anyone in the same space given I'm an only child.

I'm not going to stress for now. He and I are happy and the way we do things right now works. If at some point in the future he wants to live together, we'll cross that bridge when we get there.

Shit. I think my jambalaya is burning. BRB.

Entry #131

MAN, WORK HAS BEEN BUSY! TAXES WERE DUE THIS WEEK SO THERE WAS a good bit of stress on some loans, thankfully none of mine, but it all worked out for those involved.

So, it's Benji's birthday tomorrow but it's also Easter, so Scarlett threw him a party today to celebrate. All our friends were there, even the ones that pretty much ghosted me after I moved. Fuckers.

I only know about the party because I saw the photos on social media a few minutes ago. This is Benji's second birthday without me and it seems he is doing just fine on his own.

I don't know why I just said that. I'm not jealous, I left him; I guess I just feel a little homesick from time to time. I'm happier here than I was back home, but that doesn't mean I don't mourn the me I used to be.

Scarlett threw Benji a four twenty themed party. I need to talk to Hunter about that because that would be a bomb-ass party for us to throw sometime. Maybe next year. I just looked at the calendar and it's on a Monday, so we'll have to do it that prior Saturday… something to think about.

Anyway, Hunter just texted me that he's heading home and will be here soon. We have a cute little date night planned. We're grabbing some drinks and appetizers then heading to a late movie—probably our first time going to the movies together, now that I think about it. Going to surprise him by not wearing any underwear just in case the theater isn't crowded and we get a little handsy. Skirts = easy access, if you know what I mean.

Entry #132

MONDAY APRIL 28TH 2014

DUDE. THIS FUCKING MONTH HAS FLOWN BY! LIKE I CAN'T BELIEVE IT, WHAT the hell happened to March?

Hunter and I totally made out in the movie theater—we sat all the way in the back up at the top in the corner so we could keep an eye out. Only like six other people were there anyway and we were so far back, there's no way anyone could tell what we were doing.

By the time the movie ended, we were so turned on we didn't even make it home; we had sex in the back seat of his jeep in the middle of the parking lot and it was absolutely, fucking fantastic. Ten out of ten recommend teasing your boyfriend in an empty movie theater.

I currently have eight loans in my pipeline and three are due to close next week. I have two that I have submitted for the clear to close and the others are still in the middle stages. This has been a learning curve, not going to lie, but I'm thankful for the help and support I have as I learn this new role. I'm not sure if I want to stay in processing forever given the workload/stress, but I can definitely see myself doing it long enough to learn the ropes.

Let's just say, I'm curious to see what else this industry has to offer, but for the time being, I'm going to learn how to be the best damn processor this office has ever seen.

Lent is officially over, and I have dropped the ball on daily reading, but mostly just on the weekends. Not really sure why to be honest. Though it could be because I went from reading a romance novel to a self-help book... I have some things I want to work on for myself, and if reading books will help me gain a new perspective, then so be it. They're just not always the most exciting to read so it can take me some time to finish them.

Easter was nice. Hunter and I had breakfast with the parents and they gave us these cute little Easter baskets. I'm thankful they included Hunter, and I know he was too. Got some tasty chocolate bunnies and sugar-coated marshmallows to munch on for the next few days... plus the gift cards were a nice surprise. They gave each of us a hundred and fifty bucks! Hunter wanted to give me his, but I told him to keep it and use it on himself.

After Easter baskets, Hunter and I went back to my place and spent the day together before we went out to dinner at a steakhouse.

Yoga this morning was absolutely fantastic by the way. I've been going consistently since what, October? And my body has never looked/felt as good as it does right now. I mean shit, I thought I was toned before; I definitely am now, and I feel great. Despite the daily challenges and ups and downs from time to time, I'm proud of myself for keeping up with it. Poor elliptical barely gets used, but at least it serves as a wonderful coat hanger.

Entry #133

I HAVE OFFICIALLY CLOSED MY FIRST LOAN AS A PROCESSOR! THAT FIRST clear to close call is one I will never forget. Helping families achieve homeownership is by far one of the most rewarding experiences I have been a part of, and I'm looking forward to helping many more. Now I understand why Mom stays in the industry despite all the stress it causes.

Last week was Cinco De Mayo, so Mom took everyone from the office to a nearby Mexican restaurant for tacos and margaritas. She was cool with us drinking on the clock as long as we didn't have any more than one drink each. We all managed pretty well.

Austin and I sat next to each other; not intentionally, just ended up that way, so we caught up with each other for a little bit. We are nowhere near as close as we used to be, but honestly that's for the best.

He's excited about me moving into processing and thinks I'll enjoy it better than what I was doing before. Which I do, I enjoy solving puzzles; it's just a bit repetitive, I've noticed. We talked a little more about that and his new role responsibilities since becoming licensed, and he's enjoying himself too. We even talked about Chloe at one point and let's just say he is really cute when he's gushing about someone he likes. I'm glad they found each other.

Mother's Day was also last week. Dad spoiled Mom with breakfast in bed, so I met up with them after and we walked on the beach for a little while. The weather was decent, a slight chill, but the warmth from the sun made it all worth it. She loved her perfume, and she wants me to go with her when she gets her nails done. I bought the package for her, but I don't mind tagging along—she and I haven't had a spa day in forever; like I literally can't even remember the last time we did something like that together.

Hunter had to work the afternoon shift, but he was able to join us for dinner. He was sweet, he brought her a bouquet of flowers and a beach-scented candle. We ended up going to this place that cooks hibachi in front of you.

We all went our separate ways after. Hunter's got his final exams coming up before Memorial Day, so he's spending as much time as he can studying. I'm so excited for him, he's worked so hard for this... I know he'll be happy once it's all over.

Fuck, I need to figure out a graduation party for him!!

Entry #134

PERIODS SUCCCCCCK. THIS MONTH HAS BEEN ROUGH; I WONDER IF I HAVE another cyst or something. Trying to not think the worst though and at least I'm not pregnant.

Scarlett and Benji's engagement party has been set for Saturday, June twenty-first. Hunter and I are going to fly up there Friday night and come home Sunday afternoon. While it's going to be extremely awkward celebrating my best friend's engagement to my ex-boyfriend with both their families, I'll have Hunter by my side to get me through it. Plus, there's going to be a lot of drinking and we tend to have a lot of sex when we travel, so I think I'll be just fine.

I haven't mentioned the girlfriends' group in a while. We're actually trying to get together for Memorial Day for a river float, pending the weather, so that'll be nice to do again. I really only did it that one time last year.

Hazel's out with her boyfriend right now and Hunter's studying, so it's one of those lonely, boring nights when you want to hang out and be social but everyone around you is busy.

Probably my hormonal mood swings talking. Being around people right now does not actually seem pleasant.

Hunter and I have been texting back and forth here and there, but I'm really trying to respect his space so he can study. His exams are next Wednesday through Friday, and then he's finished until graduation on June seventh.

Man, these past few months have flown the fuck by. I really can't believe it's about to be summer… Dude… we're only a few weeks shy of me spending an entire year in the South.

So much has changed… I legit am no longer the same person I was when we first moved here. I'm so proud of myself for keeping to my promises and being open to new possibilities. Having faith truly changed my life. I'm really grateful to be where I am today.

Hunter just sent me a dick pic. He should really be studying, but at the same time I can't leave the man on read. After all, he started it.

Entry #135

DUDE.

Maybe it's my hormones, I don't know. But I can't stop thinking about my weight. It's all that's on my mind right now and it's extremely distracting because I can't focus on anything else.

I don't want to be skinny or weigh a certain amount, but there is a certain way I want to look, and while I'm good with how I look now, I want to take advantage of my youth a little better.

I don't want to blink and be forty and regret not getting my ass into gear sooner when I had the chance. I want the freedom to enjoy my thirties and the remainder of my twenties feeling confident in my own skin.

Well, maybe confident isn't the right word. Proud keeps popping in the back of my mind, so I guess that's my issue. I may be confident in my skin, but I do not feel proud because I know I am capable of taking better care of myself. I just struggle from time to time for whatever stupid fucking reason when my health gets in the way.

Damn that was heavy. But it needed to be said.

Though, that's a VERY recent discovery… I'm talking so recently, my pen can't keep up with how quickly the words are appearing in my mind. It's a beautiful thing when this happens, but it sure as fuck can hurt the heart.

Oh man. Sometimes I think I've got it all figured out, when really, I haven't got a clue. Seems the older I get, the more complicated life's problems tend to be.

Lucky me.

Entry #136

WHAT A FUCKING ROLLERCOASTER THESE PAST TWO WEEKS HAVE BEEN.

Hunter studied so hard for his exams… I'm talking study prep all day in class and then continuing at home on nights he didn't have to work. He busted his ass, and it was all totally worth it because he passed all his exams! He finally got his test results yesterday—what a tease making people wait so long.

He was so free with himself on Monday when we went floating down the river. It was nice to see him completely let loose and enjoy himself. He's such a fucking goofball. I love him.

P.S. We had sex in the river.

In the deep end away from everyone, of course.

Plus, I can't swim for shit so I stayed wrapped around him for the most part, so nobody could really tell anyway. Pretty much the usual gang was there. Hazel, Max's brother, the rest of the girls in the group with their guys, and then Hunter and me.

By the end of the float, I was definitely ready to go. The current was so damn slow, it was hot, and I was ready for a cool shower. Hunter was a bit drunk so I drove us back to his place so he could change.

For the first time ever, we showered in his bathroom together. I was using his soap to wash with and his towels to dry my body with. The tables have turned, and the view is quite intriguing.

We were most definitely late getting to Max's house for the BBQ because we had sex when we got out of the shower. He used that clit-sucking thingy on me while he was inside of me.

I was on top of him when he used it on me the first time. And I was bent over in front of him when he used it on me the second time. And yes, I was very loud.

Good thing we were running behind, because they ran out of certain ingredients. Took us two stores but we finally found one that was open so late. Got what we needed and bolted over because both Hunter and I were starving. Thankfully he was sober enough to drive, because I was getting tired from all the sun. Plus, not going to lie, he really did wear me out a good bit back at his place. Good thing his roommate wasn't home. Shit, that would have been awkward.

Shit. He moves out next week!!!!!

Entry #137

WE'RE ON THE PLANE HEADING TO NEW YORK RIGHT NOW; GOT ABOUT A two-ish hour flight, so I have some time to get caught up in here. Hunter's got a movie playing on his phone.

It's been an eventful few weeks... I really need to get back to writing more consistently, but hey, at least I'm keeping up with the times.

Hunter's sister and her husband came to town with their two kids for the week to celebrate his graduation. They had a blast together; I can tell he misses his family.

He's also really great with kids by the way. It was so hot, my ovaries were hurting.

His family is nice, and we all seemed to get along well. I was a bit nervous sitting with them during the graduation ceremony, but they all made me feel like a part of the family, so my nerves settled quickly.

Hunter looked so proud walking across the stage. He's worked so hard juggling between school and work... he deserved to shine, and brightly he did.

All seven of us went out to dinner afterward and celebrated with some drinks. I drove Hunter home and he arrived to an empty house... his roommate must have finally gotten the last of his things out. He was a little sad at first because he'll miss his friend, but then he quickly got over it when he realized we were alone within our own walls, specifically not attached to his girlfriend's parents' walls.

His house is way bigger than my space, and we absolutely took advantage of the freedom.

As a sneaky, sexy graduation surprise, I bought us bed restraints for us to use when we're here now that we'll have some legit privacy. They also double as over-the-door restraints when you crisscross them.

He decided he wanted to use them over the door first, so I took off all my clothes and he strapped me in by my ankles and wrists. Talk about X marks the spot.

We have a safe word now by the way. It's "red."

He used that clit-sucking thing on my nipples first. Then he used it on my clit and that's when my whole body started to shake up until I finally came. I am certainly his submissive in the bedroom and I am not at all mad about it.

Father's Day was this past Sunday. He and Mom had breakfast together, and then he went golfing in the afternoon, so I didn't see him until we met for dinner at this steakhouse. Hunter had to work, but he sent his best.

Hazel's birthday was on Tuesday and she's having a birthday party tomorrow. I hate to miss it, but she understands why I won't be there. We decided to have a spa day when I get back… I've been dying for a massage, maybe we can do a package deal or something?

Got about an hour left to go before we land. Not going to lie, I'm super anxious to see everyone tomorrow. Easier said than done, but I'll try not to let anything that happens this weekend get to me. After all, I'll be showing up with some sexy arm candy and everyone's going to love his accent.

Entry #138

HUNTER LEFT A LITTLE BIT AGO. I JUST FINISHED UNPACKING AND SETTLING in for the night. Let me retrace my steps so I don't miss anything.

After the plane landed, we got some dinner in us and unpacked a little, showered, and did our thing for the night.

Saturday morning, we had bagels for breakfast and slowly got ourselves together to meet Scarlett, Benji, and whoever else at the venue to help set up. Turns out both of their parents were there to help, along with Scarlett's brother. He and Hunter had fun catching up and fucking around with each other, while I helped Scarlett do whatever she needed me to do. She was so nervous. Benji, he was a total wreck making sure everything was as perfect for Scarlett as could be.

Fast forward, and lunch was catered; we had a taco bar set up, which was pretty cool. The food was good. Eventually it was time for the party and guests started to arrive around two forty-five-ish.

During the toasts, it was mentioned that Benji and Scarlett moved into their own place shortly after they got engaged... was a little surprised because you'd think Scarlett would have told me about that, so I'm not sure why she hid it from me. When I found out, I couldn't help but look at her and caught her looking back at me. I didn't want to unintention-ally ruin her day, so I just let it be. However, that was confirmation that now that they're getting married, our relationship is certainly going to change. I just hope I don't lose my best friend.

Since this was an appetizer and drinks kind of event, by the time it was over I was starving. I munched on whatever I could to get me through cleanup. After the party, we all went to Benji's parents' restaurant for dinner; they closed early so we could have the place to ourselves. This was the first time I've been back here since moving, and let's just say I felt ALL THE MOTHERFUCKING FEELINGS.

Not going to lie, I hated the memory flashbacks that I felt as soon as we pulled up to the place in our rental car. Hunter asked me what was wrong, and I was honest and told him that this wasn't just "some restaurant." Before we got out of the car, he hugged me and didn't let go until I was ready. He told me we didn't have to go inside and could leave, but I didn't want to cause a scene, so I told him we'd stay for dinner and leave not too long after. When we left it was dark out, but I wanted to show him around my old stomping grounds since we didn't have much time for that back when we were here in December.

We drove past my old house and the park I used to hang out on the swings at... even stopped for ice cream at the place around the corner. Did a little reminiscing before heading back to our hotel, though we did stop by the store on our way so we could pick up some snacks and alcohol. The party had beer and wine, so we decided to stick with that and crushed two bottles of wine together.

We got pretty drunk and moved our party into the shower. From there, we made out and had sex before fooling around more in the bed. We had a really great night together.

This morning, we were more hungover than we expected to be, so we grabbed some coffee before meeting up with Scarlett, Benji, and Scarlett's brother for breakfast. It was a little awkward, especially because all this time for the last four months, Scarlett has hidden the fact that they moved in together, for whatever reason. I decided to be the bigger person and not bring it up.

He and I pretty much got out of breakfast as fast as we could and headed to the airport after saying our goodbyes. I hope this isn't the last time I see Scarlett. I don't know anything about marriage because she's my first friend to get engaged.

Hunter and I napped as best as we could on the plane… takeoff and landing were a little shaky, but luckily by then the hangovers weren't as bad as they were. Caffeine, water, and food certainly helped.

We took my car to the airport, so I drove us back to my place. We had Chinese delivered and just kind of winded down for the night. Smoked a joint together before Hunter went home. He would have stayed the night if I didn't have work tomorrow. Since he's officially graduated, his uncle is now allowing him to transition to work full-time in the kitchen so he can start to gain more hands-on experience. From time to time when things were busy, he was asked to jump in, but now he'll be in the kitchen full-time. He's excited and I'm happy for him. I didn't know this before, but he and his uncle have spoken about Hunter taking over ownership of the bar one day, which is freaking bad ass. I know he would do very well at it.

As for me? Who knows what the future holds.

For now, I'm just going to keep learning and growing in my career while continuing to take care of my health and well-being as best as I can. It's officially been a year now that I've been living in the South, living on my own, and a year that I've known Hunter.

So much has changed…

When I look back and think about who and where I was a year ago, I just can't believe I am where I am right now. This new life of mine is something I never saw coming, and I pray it continues to move in a positive direction. I'm extremely blessed to have such caring and supportive parents who want nothing but the best for me. Without them, I would not be where I am today. I hope they know how much I appreciate them.

Entry #139

HUNTER'S BEEN ENJOYING HIS NEW ROLE WORKING IN THE KITCHEN FULL-time; he's the new prep cook. He and the head chef have been friends for years, so it's a fun change of pace getting to work more closely together. As a graduation gift to Hunter, he's going to sit down with him and see what ideas he has about switching up the menu a little bit. I could barely keep up with what he was saying, he was so excited, but his smile sure did light up the room.

I'm enjoying processing a bit more. It's still a bit repetitive, but I'm learning to focus on the backstories behind the loans instead of the conditions I'm chasing.

At the end of the day, I'm enjoying what I do because buying a house is life-changing and I get to help people do that every day. It's a rewarding experience I never would have known about if it hadn't been for Mom.

Fourth of July this year fell on a Friday, so we got off work early Thursday. The guy with the boat couldn't host this year, his parents called dibs, so we planned a camping trip instead. The camping trip consisted of myself and Hunter, Hazel, Max's brother, and Max.

Camping was a fucking blast! We each had our own tents, and we were a good distance apart, so we didn't have to be totally quiet. Even better, they had bathrooms and showers, because I'm not peeing on a leaf and washing in a bucket, no fucking way.

We did some hiking on Friday and floated down the river on Saturday. There were even fireworks both Friday and Saturday night! We didn't watch them off a boat this year; instead we watched them off a pier, wrapped around each other's arms. I say this year had to be my favorite Fourth of July ever.

When the fireworks ended, we went back to our campsite and continued to drink and talk around the bonfire. It was cozy, romantic, and the vibes were so peaceful. That was how we spent both Friday and Saturday night. Thursday was a little stressful getting everything set up and put together, but we did it before it got dark out, so that was a win.

Sunday, we dragged ass getting out of bed. Between the hangovers and nearly four-hour drive ahead of us, we were in no rush to get moving. Once everyone was showered and dressed, we packed our shit up and found the nearest coffee shop to stop and recharge.

After a quick coffee and breakfast run, we got back on the road. Luckily, we drove separately from everyone else, so the ride back was much smoother than it would have been had we all driven together. Just too many people in such a tiny space, ya know what I mean?

There was about an hour left to go when I checked the GPS to see how much longer we had to go. I turned to Hunter and asked, "So, are we heading to my place or yours?"

Without hesitation, he looked at me and replied, "How about ours? I was going to give you a key to my place this weekend, but I think it would be more fun if you moved in. So… what do you think, Lucy, will you move in with me?"

His hands were wrapped around the steering wheel, and he had such a strong and confident composure. Living together actually makes the most sense, considering how much time we already spend together.

And hey, if it doesn't work out, I do have a place I can go back to. While I hope it never comes down to that, I can take comfort in knowing I have a dependable backup.

Am I finally ready to give up my comfort zone? Am I ready to share my space? Sure, the sex would increase, but you'd also see every side to each other. I'm talking about the good, the bad, the great, and the ugly.

We pulled up to the stop sign right by our street. I turned his chin to face me and told him I would love to move in with him, and then we started making out until a car behind us honked their horn, so we moved on and pulled up to my place.

Before I went inside, I confessed that I was nervous, and so was Hunter, but we agreed to figure things out together, one step at a time. Despite the day we've had traveling back home, he's making a salad and flatbread pizzas for dinner tonight so I should really get moving. I'm not spending the night over there tonight, but we are going to chat and come up with a game plan over dinner.

◆ ◆ ◆

Wow. I can't believe I'm moving in with a guy; what am I going to tell the parents? I'm sure they'll be fine. Might be a little surprised, but it'll be okay.

I really hope to continue my routine of yoga in the mornings before work, reading, and writing. I have no idea what stuff I'll be bringing with me yet, but I think it'll be fun planning it together.

When I moved here a year ago, I did not at all see this coming.

I don't know what the future holds, but I do hope to continue filling my pages with awesome memories and bad ass stories.

What I do know for certain is that I'm going to need one thick ass notebook to write about all the new things I'll be experiencing living with a man. This is going to be so much fun, I'm so excited!

Entry #140

MONDAY JULY 7TH 2014

HUNTER AND I CAME UP WITH A SOLID MOVE IN PLAN LAST NIGHT. WE'RE going to spend the week getting ourselves together before I officially move in this weekend!

He's turning his old roommate's room into a game room, and for the third bedroom, he thinks it would be cool to turn it into a guestroom/office. He's going to take out his couch and bedroom set and replace it with mine since it's a little newer and can fit all of our stuff. He's moving his furniture into the game room and guestroom/office. And yes, I am bringing my desk with me, there's enough room.

We're going to keep his mattress for the time being, but he thinks it would be cool if we went and picked out a new one together. I personally love that idea.

Oh, and don't forget my kitchen table, that's coming with us and will replace the one he has now. He likes the height better on mine, which I am totally fine with considering how great it is for sex. Even my purple table is coming! That's going in the backyard, which is a fairly nice size by the way. As for the rest of our appliances and dishes, we're going to mesh them together and see what we get. I am going to leave my washer and dryer behind though; neither one of us feels like moving it and his are fairly new anyway. We worked things out way easier than I expected, and I'm excited to see how we end up setting things up.

The countdown is officially on! He's taking off from work Friday through Sunday so we can get all of my things moved in and settled.

I had dinner with the parents tonight and shared the news with them. They were a little surprised at first, but overall, they're excited for me. They're cool with me keeping some things in my current space and said it'll always be there for me if I needed it. Mom even gave me the day off on Friday so I can have an extra day to get settled in before Monday.

I'm honestly super nervous, but I have a feeling it'll all be okay. Plus, Hunter has two bathrooms sooo one for each of us! That'll make bathroom time way easier for me.

FUCK ME, this is going to be quite an adjustment. I haven't even thought about the whole bathroom situation. I've only been fantasizing about the idea of dinners, sex, and spending every morning and night together.

Entry #141

THURSDAY JULY 10ᵀᴴ 2014

WELL, JUST ABOUT ALL OF MY THINGS ARE PACKED UP.

Tonight's my last night sleeping in my bed alone, in my own place.

I can't freakin' believe this. My entire life has changed within fourteen months and trying to piece it all together just feels like pure insanity.

In a good way, obviously.

So much is racing through my mind, but I'm staying positive because let's be real here, Hunter and I pretty much spend all of our free time together anyway, so this is nothing different.

I told Hazel about it earlier in the week and she immediately mentioned wedding bells—she thinks it's only a matter of time before Hunter proposes. I think that might be a little fast, but honestly, she's known him way longer than I have, and it's not like I would say no if he asked.

Fuck, I'm getting WAY ahead of myself right now. I need to focus on one major milestone at a time before I lose my mind. I need to figure out how to adjust to living with a man before I even think about being someone's wife.

I can't believe tonight is the last time I'll be locking my own doors and settling in for the night on my own. I may not have lived in this house for very long, but I've done a lot of growing up here.

I almost wonder if moving here is what helped me find myself?

Entry #142

IT TOOK A FEW TRIPS, BUT WE MANAGED TO GET ALL MY THINGS OUT OF my place and over to his. Ours.

Wait, when is it okay to update my driver's license?!

I took one more walk around my place alone before driving over to Hunter's to be officially moved in. Not going to lie, I was in my feelings for a minute before walking in, but after I saw a glimpse of him in the front windows, I instantly knew everything was going to be okay.

When I walked through the front door, Hunter was messing with some things in the living room. Seeing our stuff together under one roof was one of the best feelings I have ever felt. And knowing we get to wake up and go to sleep together every night feels like a dream come true.

We had pizza delivered for dinner so we could finish getting everything settled. Nearly close to midnight, all of my clothes were unpacked, his game room was set up, and the living room was put back together. All we have left to do now is go through dishes, kitchen stuff, and home décor.

I'm definitely going to be burning candles all the time. He better be ready for that, is all I'm sayin.

Oh, I brought my elliptical with me, it's in the office/guestroom. We're thinking about getting a pull-out couch to put in there so it doesn't look like a bedroom. Which is totally fine by me; I think it's a much better idea than putting an entire bed in there.

Waking up together Saturday morning hit differently than it ever has. We woke up together for the first time in OUR home.

We absolutely had sex to celebrate. I woke up to him cuddling up against me, then the next thing I knew, he was under the covers with his head between my legs.

Morning head perk unlocked.

I don't know where that came from but I'm hoping it's here to stay.

Hunter didn't want head, he just wanted to be inside of me, so I got on all fours and he fucked me from behind. He even reached around and played with me again; I'm totally digging that new vibe.

We spent Saturday going through our things and deciding what to keep and what to toss. Honestly didn't even leave the house all day. Around lunchtime he made us chicken and beef quesadillas while I sorted through our things and got acquainted with the cabinets. I rearranged them after adding in all my things and I had a lot of fun doing it.

I can't help it, I like to organize things sometimes. It's soothing. Hunter mentioned he's the same way.

We had some groceries delivered for dinner so we didn't have to go anywhere. He made us shrimp tortellini alfredo with a Caesar salad on the side. This man is going to spoil me with nice meals, I'm so fucking excited.

For breakfast this morning, we sixty-nined on the dining room table while the coffee was brewing. Yep, you read that right. What a fucking way to start a Sunday!

We actually left the house today and bought a new mattress; it'll be here sometime next week. We also bought a BBQ so we can start grilling.

Hunter wanted to pay for the mattress, so I paid for the BBQ. Since he doesn't have a mortgage on the house, I'm going to give him three hundred dollars a month to contribute towards bills. That includes the water, electricity, Wi-Fi, cable, property taxes, and homeowners' insurance. And as far as groceries go, we'll rotate and split those.

OMG I almost forgot to write about the moment Hunter gave me my key! I'm not sure when he had it made for me, but when I walked in the door Friday night, he had the bed made with this cute little white square box wrapped in a purple bow sitting on my pillow. When I opened it up, there was my house key attached to a keychain with a charm on it in the shape of a house. I legit almost cried, it was the sweetest thing ever and I love that he did that for me.

Tomorrow starts our new reality of living together. I've got yoga in the morning, so I've got to get up a little earlier than he does. I wonder what he's like when he's getting ready for work? Sure, he's left from my place before, but this is totally different. Here he's in his own comfort zone.

Shit. It's really getting late. It's ten fifty-eight and I want to be able to spend some time with him before we go to bed.

Fuck. I can't believe Hunter and I are officially living together. This time last year, we were walking along the shoreline at his friends' parents' beach house, wanting nothing more than to hold each other's hand. Crazy how we were both feeling the same way but had no idea.

I guess it's true when they say things happen when they do for a reason. He and I had to blossom the way we did to understand who we are as individuals and who we want to be together. I needed to find myself and that's exactly what he gave me the space to do. He's been nothing but supportive from the very beginning and I'm just so grateful to have met him.

Shit! I almost forgot. He bought me a new notebook! He knew this one was low.

It's a teal-blue spiral notebook with "Home Sweet Home" written in the center of the cover and a cottage-style house pictured in the middle, wrapped in a floral wreath. It's perfect and I absolutely love it. I can't wait to fill it with our next set of adventures.

It's only been forty-eight hours and I can already feel in my heart that this is going to work out. I may still have my head in the clouds from the high of us moving in together, but this man knows me so well—maybe even better than I know myself sometimes.

We've totally got this!

Acknowledgments

First, I would like to give a huge shout out to my beta readers for sticking with me through my second book.I thought the first one was nerve-wracking, but boy was I in for a surprise when I introduced book number two. I appreciate each and every one of you for putting up with my anxiety and constant questions.

To my husband, Tim. Thank you for continuing to support me through-out my writing journey and for helping spread the word of all things *Chasing My Twenties*. Having you in my corner is one of the biggest blessings in my life. Thank you for always believing in me.

I also would like to thank the team at Publish Pros for all of their help, support, and guidance. They took the time to walk me through every single one of my questions, for which I am extremely grateful for. Thank you for bringing my vision for book two to life!

To my current and future readers, I thank you from the bottom of my heart for your support. I truly appreciate each and every one of you for showing my books so much love!